BEVERLY HILLS PUBLIC LIBRARY
P9-BJC-620
3 5048 00240 4346

SPREADING POISON

OTHER BOOKS BY JOHN LANGONE

AIDS
The Facts

Bombed, Buzzed, Smashed, or . . . Sober
A Book about Alcohol

Dead End
A Book about Suicide

Death Is a Noun
A View of the End of Life

Goodbye to Bedlam
Understanding Mental Illness and Retardation

Growing Older
What Young People Should Know about Aging

Human Engineering
Marvel or Menace?

Life at the Bottom
The People of Antarctica

Like, Love, Lust
A View of Sex and Sexuality

Long Life
What We Know and Are Learning about the Aging Process

Our Endangered Earth
What We Can Do to Save It

Thorny Issues
How Ethics and Morality Affect the Way We Live

Violence!
Our Fastest-Growing Health Problem

Vital Signs
The Way We Die in America

SPREADING POISON

A Book about Racism and Prejudice

by John Langone

Little, Brown and Company
Boston Toronto London

For Matthew and Lynn

First Edition

Library of Congress Cataloging-in-Publication Data
Langone, John, 1929–
Spreading poison : a book about racism and prejudice / John Langone. — 1st ed.
p. cm.
Summary: Discusses the history of various racial and ethnic groups in the United States, including contributions made despite biases, and examines the problem of religious and sexual discrimination.
ISBN 0-316-51410-1
1. Racism — United States — Juvenile literature. 2. Prejudices — United States — Juvenile literature. 3. United States — Race relations — Juvenile literature. 4. United States — Ethnic relations — Juvenile literature. [1. Racism. 2. Prejudices. 3. Minorities.]
I. Title.
E184.A1L258 1993
305.8′00973 — dc20 92-17847

10 9 8 7 6 5 4 3 2 1

RRD-VA

Published simultaneously in Canada
by Little, Brown & Company (Canada) Limited

Printed in the United States of America

CONTENTS

INTRODUCTION
Understanding — and Fighting — the Roots of Prejudice

It is never too late to give up
your prejudices.
— Henry David Thoreau, *Walden*

Each and every one of us has strong likes and dislikes. The object of our affection or our distaste may be something or somebody. We might crave chocolate because of the great taste but be repelled by raw oysters because we don't like the way they look or because we tried them once and they almost made us sick. We like a certain hairstyle because it's flattering, dislike another because it makes us look weird. Some of us like rock and rap but don't like Dixieland jazz. Some books we'll return to again and again; others we read only because they are assigned. We like and don't like certain films, styles of clothes, and sports. We have favorite teachers and performers, and we have friends. We know people we don't care to hang out with. There are even people whom we hate.

It may seem easy to explain the way we feel about something. Things, from oysters to perfumes to jogging shoes to music, have a direct effect on our five senses. So if we enjoy the way something tastes, smells, looks, feels, or sounds, we can say that we like it; if something offends one sense or another, we make a negative judgment about it.

But with people, it is a bit more difficult to explain why we feel the way we do toward them. True, we can sometimes rely on some of the five senses: we might like someone because he or she is attractive or sexy to us or has a great voice or wears the right perfume or cologne, and we may not like someone whom we think unattractive or smells bad or has an irritating laugh. But there is far more behind our feelings for people, and the reasons we like or dislike someone are a complex mix of psychology, heredity, and our upbringing.

Sometimes, too, a sixth sense, intuition, is at work in the way we respond to people. Intuition is a hunch, a gut feeling, that seems to tell us instantly how to feel and act. We like some people instantly; others we dislike just as fast. But if we tried to explain why, we'd be at a loss. "I just like him — that's all," we might say, or, "She just turns me off."

The power of the sixth sense is as great as that of the five other senses, and it is often right on the mark in helping us pick friends or make some other kind of choice. Other times, though, the voice of intuition may be silent. So we can't always rely on it to tell us whom we should like or dislike, no more than we can rely on pure luck to give us what we want. In the absence of intuition's sudden insight, which has no reasoning behind it, we have to do some real, solid thinking when we start considering people. Remember, though, that our reasoning process is influenced and even directed by many people and events, by books we read and movies we see, by what our religious faith and our schools teach us, by our memories, and by our own self-interest and needs. Our brains are the computers that process all this information, using some very intricate mechanisms to sift through piles of data, advice, and other people's experiences. Then we weight it all and come up with an answer that feels comfortable.

But even all this reasoning has its flaws. Reasoning does not necessarily lead to the right answer. If the information in our data bases is flawed, so, too, will be the conclusions our mental computers spit out. Too often, in fact, errors creep into our thinking — errors in the form of prejudices and biases — and these color our reasoning process. Anger and passion sometimes intrude as well. When our brains are short-circuited by all these elements, we fail to see the good in people. Our judgment becomes shaky, unreliable, and ultimately, wrong. As the French philosopher René Descartes said, "The chief cause of human errors is to be found in the prejudices picked up in childhood."

Let's consider some of the reasons we like or dislike some people. And as we do, ask yourself whether the reasons are good ones. We might, for example, like people who give us a lot of praise or who are smart, wealthy, or successful. We also tend to like people who do things for us. For instance, we may like the person who always pays for the burgers, who helps us with our homework, or who has a car — or a brother who works at the local movie theater and can get us in for free. We like certain teachers because they don't demand a lot from the class. Sometimes we pick a friend because he or she is always ready to listen to our troubles and seems to have the right answers; sometimes we make the choice because that person shares our interests or because he or she always agrees with our views. We might also favor people who share our religious beliefs, who have the same skin color as ours, the same nationality, the same educational background, or the same amount of money. We are comfortable with such people. They are kindred spirits. We do not have to learn about them. They are not mysterious or strange, and so we do not fear them as we do those whom we know little or nothing about. We trust them more than we do "outsiders."

We may *dis*like people for all the opposite reasons. We tend to avoid people who criticize our work, our behavior, or our appearance. We may dislike anyone who has wronged us or said unkind things about us or who refuses to do us a favor or listen to our problems. We are suspicious or fearful of people we have had little contact with, who have a "reputation" of committing violent acts, are mentally unbalanced, worship some "strange" god, or have sexual habits unlike ours.

Liking and disliking people for some of the reasons we've mentioned is understandable, and may even be okay. The extent to which someone either rewards or punishes us is not always a bad guide when we're making choices about people; neither are the various qualities, beliefs, and accomplishments that attract us to some people and cause us to avoid others. When people are always critical of us in a destructive way, we shouldn't have to take it. The same goes for people who never ever go out of their way for us and never seem to have the time to listen. Most of us don't want to associate with people who lead a life of crime or are emotionally disturbed. We also may believe so strongly in our own religion and hold such strict views of sex that any practice but the one we are used to is unacceptable.

But this book is not about normal dislikes, the rational, acceptable reasons we don't care for some people. It is about irrational disliking, about angry, passionate, unreasoned attitudes directed against individuals, against groups of individuals, and against races and their supposed characteristics. It is a book about that irrational hostility we call prejudice.

Prejudice and racism — the belief that one's race determines human traits and capabilities and that racial differences are what make us superior or inferior — are among the most important issues that teenagers must consider. Both affect not only the way we regard others, but in the long run, our *relationships* with others. Because of prejudice and racism, we develop stereotypes, oversimplified mental images of people that are as cruel as they are unfair. Stereotypes are difficult to get rid of because as we keep learning, believing, and voicing them, they become part of our thinking processes and those of the people around us. Eventually, truth is buried, and falsehood becomes the accepted view.

You don't have to go very far to see or hear evidence of prejudice and racism. It is in your schools, in your neighborhood, perhaps even in your homes. You can see graphic examples of these crimes against humanity on your television screens, and you can read about them in your daily newspapers. We learn of blacks denied education and jobs because of their color, of blacks picketing Korean-run grocery stores, of Italian-Americans fending off the stereotype of membership in the Mafia. We hear of country clubs that bar nonwhites, of apartheid in South Africa, of Parisians desecrating Jewish cemeteries, of young skinheads screaming white supremacy, of meetings of the Ku Klux Klan, of Arab-Americans threatened in the wake of the Gulf War, even of the FBI singling out black officials for harassment and prosecution. Because of the awful disease AIDS, which has infected many homosexuals, we hear hysterical anti-gay remarks and read that violence against gays is on the increase. Women are sexually harassed on the job by men or are denied promotion or are paid less simply because, although no one except the women will say it, they are women. Older workers are laid off or fired or forced to retire before they want to simply because — and again no one except the workers will admit it — they are not young.

And there are the many epithets, insulting words or phrases. It is doubtful that any group of people or religion is without one or more. You probably know most of them and have maybe even used some of them: kike, wop, dago, guinea, wetback, dyke, faggot, queer, harp, honkie, nigger, redneck, gook, limey, Polack, kraut, frog, spick, holy roller, goy, broad, chink, Jap, slope, Portugee, bead squeezer, spaghetti bender, herring choker, mackerel snapper. There are also the jokes about how many Italians (or "Polacks" or Swedes) it takes to change a light bulb, the references to dirty old men and old geezers, old maids and old hags. Sad to say, when someone calls us one of the names from the list above, we often respond with another epithet, the idea being to hurt that person back.

If what you have just read makes you wince and feel uncomfortable, that's a good sign. If you dismiss it or laugh, you need to do some thinking. Ethnic humor is not what we are arguing against here. Every group of people has traits and displays behavior that can be funny or the subject of a caricature or a satire. The people within that group are usually aware of those qualities, and unless they are overly sensitive, they are generally able to laugh at themselves and even laugh when someone not a member of their group mocks them. It is when someone who generally does not belong to their group applies an epithet out of malice, out of habit, or out of ignorance that it becomes a matter of concern.

Malice, habit, ignorance. Three key contributors to prejudice and racism. If we are white and don't know any blacks, or the only ones we hear about are the ones who are arrested for committing crimes, we may argue that all blacks are to be avoided; if we are black and have been directly mistreated by whites or cannot forget what we have read about how whites treated black slaves, we may resent whites. If we have money, we may be disgusted by poor people and may believe all of them are poor because they're lazy; if we are poor, we may think all people who are rich are dishonest and selfish. Some men believe that women belong only at home, that they shouldn't be out competing for the same jobs as men because they aren't as capable at certain tasks as men. Depending on our religious affiliation, we might be convinced that Catholics cannot think for themselves and take all their orders from the pope; that Jews are interested only in money; that "WASPs" (white Anglo-Saxon Protestants) are all privileged, haughty, and self-serving; or that all Muslims are terrorists. If we are heterosexual, we might believe that all gay men have AIDS.

In the pages ahead, we will examine many different kinds of prejudice — racial, religious, and sexual — and we'll look at how they have been expressed throughout history. You will learn of the many contributions made by the people who have been the most frequent victims of prejudice. With enough correct information, your attitudes — if they are flawed — can be changed so that your prejudices will disappear. This is important not only because it will make you a better, more understanding person and widen your circle of friends, but it will prevent you from fostering discrimination — that process by which we treat someone favorably or unfavorably because of national origin, religion, sex, politics, or philosophy. One day, each of you will probably be called upon to choose one person over another for a job or perhaps even as a wife or husband. It is hoped that some of what you read here will help you make the best choice when that day comes.

Each of us is a unique individual, a product of our genes and our environment. The genes you have inherited from your parents and other ancestors have shaped some of your attitudes as well as your appearance. So, too, does the environment in which you live — the relatives, teachers, and friends whom you observe and who, either by their own behavior or by their advice, have a great deal of influence over your likes and dislikes.

If those influences have put you on the wrong track, it's tough to get off it. Not impossible, however. Sometimes all it takes is a little common sense, that straightforward, quite ordinary form of judgment, to stop prejudice before it starts boiling in your head. Once you understand how sick prejudice and racism are, you can stop them from doing damage by taking the next step — speaking out loudly and clearly against them. Maybe after reading some of the history of prejudice that we'll present, after you digest some of the more appalling consequences of it — the organized massacres of helpless people in pogroms and during the Holocaust, the lynchings of blacks by the Ku Klux Klan, the internment of Japanese-Americans in the United States during World War II, our mistreatment of Native Americans, to name but a few examples — it will be easy for you to do the right thing.

1 • RACE AND RACISM
Exploding the Myth of Racial Purity

Let every man honor and love the land of his birth and the race from which he springs and keep their memory green.

— Henry Cabot Lodge

Race is a word we use often, and loosely. The human race. The races of mankind. The savage race. The superior race. The inferior race. The white, black, and yellow races.

But what does *race* actually mean? We should first establish what it is not. *Race* is not a term that describes an Italian, a Spaniard, a Swede, or any other nationality; the languages these people speak and their special habits come from the society in which they were born and reared, no matter what their race. *Race* does not necessarily refer to a geographically defined population —that is, to all people who live on one continent or other or in a particular country — because people often move around and mingle in places far from home. Nor does *race* define a religious group. Jews, for example, are people who follow the teachings of the Jewish religion, and Muslims are people who practice Islam; Jews and Muslims can be of all races. And *race* does not apply only to people who make pottery or eat with their fingers or dance in feathered bonnets. Hundreds of years ago, people of different races in many different places wore feathers, made pots, and ate without forks and knives.

All human beings belong to a particular race, a group that shares certain distinctive biological and physical characteristics. Skin and eye color, hair texture, and the shape of a nose are all used to divide humans into different races. These physical attributes are the result of heredity.

Anthropologists generally recognize three human races: Caucasian, or white; Negroid, or black; and Mongoloid, or yellow. Other scientists say there are many more races, including Native American and Australian aborigine. There are also many subdivisions within the three generally accepted races. For example, the Nordics, from northern Europe, make up a group within the Caucasian race; the Alpines, from central Europe, form another; and the Mediterraneans, from southern Europe, constitute still another.

Race theory is a tricky subject, but several aspects of it are fairly clear. One is that all of the races we know sprang, in all probability, from a common ancestral background. This means that all humans belong to one species, *Homo sapiens,* a Latin term meaning wise man. Because all races share a common ancestor, they have more features in common than they do differences.

Another important fact about race is that a "pure" race is virtually impossible. Centuries ago, people lived in isolated tribes, and through inbreeding, they acquired various physical characteristics. It was these characteristics that enabled scientists to separate the various tribes and families into races. It is rather like drawing lines on a map to divide states and countries.

The map analogy is important when we talk about so-called racial purity. The lines that divide our states and the world's countries are imaginary, human inventions. They are not physical barriers, like a brick wall that prevents someone from walking across a border. Racial categories are also human inventions, and though they are based on fairly specific biological and physical characteristics, no real barriers, no brick walls, separate the categories. For centuries, people of various races have been moving about, intermarrying, and sharing each other's cultural and social lives. Thus, at least among the industrialized nations of the world, most people are racially mixed, Americans and Europeans being the most blended of all. Centuries ago, Moors from northern Africa overran Spain and moved into France; Greeks, Romans, barbarians, and Normans all occupied southern Italy at various times; Spanish and Native American have combined in Mexico and in South and Central America; a Hawaiian may have a mixture of Caucasian, Chinese, Japanese, Portuguese, and Polynesian blood; Angolans may be black and Portuguese; Cubans and Puerto Ricans, black and Spanish; Polynesians are combinations of Negroid, Mongoloid, and Caucasian.

It is, therefore, not only very difficult to find a person of pure race in the world, but it is difficult to classify races at all, and it is impossible to use one trait or another to define a race. None of us knows how many racial mixes have made us what we are as individuals, no matter how far back we can trace our personal genealogies. Looking for coats of arms and for our "roots" is a worthwhile pursuit, but we can take it only so far. If we could take the search all the way back to the dawn of history, we'd find that there is but one race, the human one.

Despite all of the difficulties and uncertainties about race, people — including scientists — continue to try to pigeonhole, to classify, all the varieties of human beings on earth. But placing too much emphasis on human variation can be a dangerous course, because it may breed racism, the belief that race is chiefly what determines a person's traits and abilities and that racial differences produce an inherited superiority or inferiority.

Consider the following, written during World War I, more than seventy-five years ago, by Henry Fairfield Osborn, a professor of zoology at Columbia University:

> Whatever may be its intellectual, its literary, its artistic or its musical aptitudes, as compared with other races, the Anglo-Saxon branch of the Nordic race is again showing itself to be that upon which the nation must chiefly depend for leadership, for courage, for loyalty, for unity and harmony of action, for self-sacrifice and devotion to an ideal. Not that members of other races are not doing their part, many of them are, but in no other human stock which has come to this country is there displayed the unanimity of

> heart, mind and action which is now being displayed by the descendants of the blue-eyed, fair-haired peoples of the north of Europe.[1]

That not-so-subtle racist philosophy of history is found in the preface of an equally disturbing book, *The Passing of the Great Race.* Written by Madison Grant, who was chairman of the New York Zoological Society and a trustee of the American Museum of Natural History, it is an absurd tract on the myth of Nordic racial supremacy, one that has been widely criticized by generations of anthropologists and sociologists. In his book, Grant warned that the Nordics were engaged in a last battle against the inferior races pouring into America from southern and eastern Europe. He wrote:

> We Americans must realize that the altruistic ideals which have controlled our social development during the past century and the maudlin sentimentalism that has made America "an asylum for the oppressed," are sweeping the nation toward a racial abyss. If the melting pot is allowed to boil without control and we continue to follow our national motto and deliberately blind ourselves to all "distinctions of race, creed or color," the type of native American of Colonial descent will become as extinct as the Athenian of the age of Pericles, and the Viking of the days of Rollo.[2]

Grant's use of the term "native American of Colonial descent," makes one wonder what American Indians, who have lived here since long before the colonials and Columbus arrived, would have thought had they read such nonsense. Works like Madison's are, however, more than just embarrassing. They give plenty of ammunition to racists who are eager to prove that they are superior to other groups of people. They give rise to theories that try to prove that people of certain races are mentally inferior. What Madison and others preached so fervently was the same sort of rubbish that Adolf Hitler relied on to justify the eradication of "mentally defective" people and Jews and to perpetuate the myth of an Aryan "master race." *Aryan* is another word that is thrown around loosely by racists. It originally referred to a prehistoric people who may have come from Russia and who spread through India and Europe. However, *Aryan* now refers not to a race but to a family of languages that includes the major European ones. The false belief that a superior Aryan race existed was seized on by Hitler and his Nazis, who deluded themselves into thinking that they were a branch of this "pure" race and were not only responsible for civilizing Europe but were also the rightful rulers of the world.

Today's new Nazis might not like to hear about it, but it seems that the original Aryan peoples were not all blonds with blue eyes, characteristics which, in the minds of many racists, mark a superior individual. Folktales from India often describe the early Aryans as dark-haired and dark-eyed. Moreover, the unwritten language of Muslim Kurds, who live in the highlands of Turkey and neighboring regions, belongs to the Aryan language group, as does Yiddish, the dialect spoken by many Jews. Thus, a Kurdish-speaking Muslim and a Yiddish-speaking Jew are as Aryan in language as anyone who speaks German or English.[3]

Does race dictate how smart someone is? Or whether someone becomes a criminal?

There is no firm evidence that one race is intellectually superior to another, although a number of scientists believe that since some inherited diseases seem to plague certain races more than others — sickle-cell anemia among blacks, for instance — then it follows that perhaps intelligence, and even criminal behavior, may also be connected to race. Recently, two professors at the City College of New York, one white, the other black, touched off a furor with their views on race and genetics. The white professor, Michael Levin, wrote that on the average, blacks "are significantly less intelligent than whites" and that this has been confirmed over several decades. The black professor, Leonard Jeffries, Jr., believes that the skin pigment, melanin, that blacks have gives them physical and neurological advantages over whites.[4]

Such claims, based on the fact that many physical and mental abnormalities and some human behavior are imprinted in our genes, can sow the seeds of racial prejudice when they are overblown, as the views of men like Madison Grant and Adolf Hitler were. Arguments that humans are shaped solely by their genes lead also to the misguided idea that superpeople can be created by putting the right genes together. By selectively mating individuals with admirable qualities, goes the argument, and by preventing "inferior" people from mating, a race or breed of people can be improved. This approach is known as eugenics, a term coined in 1883 by the English scientist Sir Francis Galton. Galton was a cousin of the famed naturalist Charles Darwin, who gave us classic theories about evolution and the results of inbreeding. It was Galton's belief that if society were to excel, it had to cultivate only the most desirable talents and suppress all undesirable traits. Galton de-emphasized the effects of social environment and focused on inherited characteristics — a perspective that was misunderstood and exaggerated by Hitler, who wanted to exterminate all people who did not fit his model of perfection.

The debate over whether nature or nurture — heredity or environmental factors — governs our behavior and our intelligence is an old one that has yet to come down hard on one side or the other. We all know of families in which an accomplished father or mother produce an outstanding child. The composer Wolfgang Amadeus Mozart was one such offspring, a child prodigy whose father was a celebrated and skilled violinist and concertmaster. Was young Mozart so talented because his father passed that talent along biologically? No one can say. Many children grow up in similar artistic or intellectual environments but do not imitate their parents. About all we can say for certain is that both heredity and environment are at work, in some mysterious proportion, in every human being, regardless of race. Every race on earth has brilliant members as well as average and below-average members. If intellectual capacity were based purely on a genetic blueprint, there would be well-defined differences among the races, and this is just not so. When people are educated properly, there is no reason why they cannot learn — unless they have some mental disability — no matter what racial group they belong to. Some people may not be able to learn because their lives are in a turmoil or because they do not have access to quality education. To believe otherwise discounts all the evidence that poverty, despair, and lack of education are as important in intellectual growth as heredity.

By the same token, a person's race doesn't dictate whether he or she will become a criminal. "All students of criminology agree that behavior is socially conditioned," says a classic textbook on criminology,

> except in individual cases where a unique biological history induces abnormal behavior traits. Therefore most antisocial behavior in minority groups arises from a conflict of the diverse cultures in which the members of such groups are enmeshed. This is notably true of the American Negro as well as of the various nationality groups whose mores differ widely from those of the old American stock.[5]

This is an important point because we hear so much today about black criminals and Italian Mafia murderers. Simply being black or Italian does not set someone up for a life of crime. If that were true, all blacks and Italians would be at risk, a presumption that is not only racist but preposterous. That doesn't mean that people haven't tried to explain criminal behavior scientifically, just as they've tried to put intelligence under a microscope. In the early 1800s, Franz Gall, a German doctor, attempted to link the shape of a person's head to violent behavior. His theory was known as phrenology, but it was discredited. (Not everyone agreed. For many years, Russian scientists studied the brains of Soviet leaders Joseph Stalin and Vladimir Ilyich Lenin — the brains are stored in a laboratory known as the Brain Institute of Moscow — in a futile effort to confirm Stalin's belief that the secret to why some people become prominent and powerful would be found inside the skull.) After Gall, an Italian criminologist, Cesare Lombroso, tried to show that criminals were born that way and that they could be identified by certain physical characteristics. He contended, for example, that the typical crook had a sloping forehead, like that of an ape, as well as large earlobes, an unpronounced chin, and either a lot of body hair or none at all. That crazy theory was also dismissed fairly quickly.

Other scientists tried to establish that Italian-Americans and Germans were at the top of the list of murderers, that Polish-Americans led in assaults, that Scandinavians were first in sex offenses and crimes involving fraud and forgery, and that Spaniards and Mexicans were more apt to possess firearms and be bootleggers, that is, criminals who made and sold liquor illegally. Again, such notions went up in the smoke of imagination. People from some of the ethnic groups in the list may well have been involved in certain crimes more often than people from other groups, but few scientists believe that it was heritage that made these criminals behave the way they did. "Crime is not due to race," concluded Dr. Earnest Hooton, a famous Harvard anthropologist who many years ago assessed the relationship between crime and racial factors.

> Every race is criminalistic, and within every race it is the biologically inferior — the organically unadaptable, the mentally and physically stunted and warped, and the sociologically warped — who are responsible for the majority of the crimes committed. Each race has its special abilities and its quota of weaknesses. Each produces its pitifully few men of genius, its hordes of the mediocre, its masses of morons, and from the very dregs of its germ plasm, its regiments of criminals.[6]

Those words still hold true. Race is a convenient way to classify groups of people, even though the classifications may not be as easy to make today as they once were. But race is not the measure of a person, and when we use it for that, we are on very shaky scientific ground. Beneath our different skins, we have many similarities. We all have hearts and minds, assets and liabilities, and tendencies toward good and evil. When we can accept that there is really but one race, the human race, we will have taken an important step toward eradicating the disease of racism.

2 • AFRICAN-AMERICANS
Unwilling Immigrants

I have a dream that my four little children will one day live in a nation where they will not be judged by the color of their skin, but by the content of their character.

— Dr. Martin Luther King, Jr.

The Negro is inferior and will remain so. This is a white man's country.

— Thomas Pearce Bailey, Dean of Education at the University of Mississippi, 1914

The White Dog, a little-known movie that made a brief appearance ten years ago, features a white German shepherd who has been trained by white bigots to attack only blacks.

Dogs are not racist by nature. To them, or any other animal, the color of someone's skin is not a signal to suddenly turn vicious. Dogs do not think as humans do, nor have they learned to be racist, as many of us have, at an early age and in an environment that teaches racism by word and deed.

Why do people hate others because of skin color? Do some whites attack blacks because, like the white dog of the movie, they are conditioned to respond to the color alone? Is it really just the color they hate, or is it something more?

It does seem odd that skin color alone should cause the rift that exists between blacks and whites — the segregation, the anger, and the violence. But then, colors have become symbols for many things. Blue sometimes represents peace and hope, red may stand for martyrdom or love, green for joy and abundance. White and black, too, have meaning. White quite often signifies truth, purity, and innocence. But black has come to signify evil, lies, mistakes. You may have heard of the nickname given to Edward, Prince of Wales, eldest son of King Edward III: the Black Prince. According to the French historian, Jean Froissart (1400), he was called that because he was "black by the terror of his arms." The Black Sea got its name because of the dangers around it. We have the terms *blackguard,* meaning a scoundrel, the *Black Death* for the bubonic plague that ravaged Europe in the Middle Ages, *black sheep* for the person who disgraces his family, and the *Black Mass,* in which the devil takes the place of God.

The point is that for some bigots, black skin can be a stimulus, a trigger. To them, like the white dog in the film, the color black represents something ominous, something that should be avoided or attacked. When a white person is uncomfortable around black people, chances are it's because he or she has a preconceived notion of blacks. And that notion is usually a stereotype. Some whites believe, for instance, that all blacks are criminals or hostile toward whites. These whites have been conditioned to expect the worst.

The Russian scientist Ivan Pavlov demonstrated how conditioning works. Pavlov knew that dogs, like humans, salivate at the sight or taste of food, and he decided to look more closely at the response. He repeatedly offered his dogs food while he rang a bell, and their mouths watered. Pavlov kept it up, ringing the bell each time he showed the dogs food. After a while, he noticed that all he had to do to make the dogs salivate was just ring the bell. No food, just the bell. The bell was the stimulus, and the mouth watering was the conditioned response.

When people make fast judgments about blacks, they do so without knowing anything about the people of "that color," and it has caused the black populations of many countries much grief, especially in countries such as Italy and Japan, where blacks stand out more than they do in our country.

Snap judgments are sometimes understandable, and appropriate, when they are applied to individual situations. Suppose for instance you are walking down a long, deserted street. If you are white, and you see a gang of black youths loitering at the corner, you might become apprehensive. You might have the same feeling if you are black and you encounter a suspicious-looking group of whites. But it is the potential danger of the situation that should concern you, not the color of the loiterers. When someone looks dangerous, it is prudent to avoid him. Snap judgments become dangerous when they are automatically made about an entire group of people. Because so many entertainers and sports figures are black, whites might think that that's all blacks can aspire to. Because so many blacks live below the poverty level and are on welfare, whites might believe that most blacks are on welfare, and like it that way. Because our prisons are overloaded with blacks, whites might think that blacks are more apt to be criminals than whites. A recent survey of whites conducted by the National Opinion Research Center at the University of Chicago found that 78 percent of the respondents thought blacks are more likely to prefer living on welfare. Sixty-two percent believed that blacks are less likely to work hard than whites, 55 percent thought blacks more violence-prone, 53 percent thought blacks less intelligent than whites, and 51 percent thought them to be less patriotic. If more than half of a large group of people have such opinions, it means that stereotypes about blacks are still very much with us.[1]

These stereotypes are not a new phenomenon in America. They probably began when our country was very young, when the first blacks, called Negroes then, were brought from Africa to Virginia in 1619 as slaves. Among the first slave traders were the Portuguese in the 1400s, and the trade became big business for all the countries that had explored and established colonies in the New World. It was a horrid business. Slaves were separated from their families and forced to travel across the ocean, sometimes chained, in the stinking holds of old ships that were often unseaworthy. Once they arrived at their destinations, the slaves were inspected and sold like cattle at slave auctions. From Virginia, slavery soon spread to the other states. Colonial slaves were forced to work for white masters, who made all the rules and were sometimes cruel. Whipping, chaining, and branding of slaves were generally prohibited by law, but these practices continued because many slave masters felt that Negroes were inferior beings that didn't deserve or require any basic human rights. Some slave owners were afraid to give slaves any rights or education because they might become "uppity" and rebel or run away. Since slavery itself was legal, it was no wonder that the slave masters felt they could treat their slaves as they pleased.

Slavery left a stain on our country that is still visible today, more than 125 years after it was abolished. Every other racial or ethnic group that has come to the United States did so voluntarily, seeking freedom and better job opportunities. Blacks were forced to come here and were stripped of their freedom in order to make life better for the people they had to serve. They were, ironically, among the first Americans, but they had few of the rights accorded other Americans. Even Native Americans, the oldest residents of our country, owned property and were free to roam wherever they pleased and govern themselves before they were driven out of their land by whites. Blacks were hostages in a nation that had welcomed other people from foreign countries. Their native culture was ignored, and their contributions, apart from the chores they were required to perform, were not taken seriously. They were thrown into the great melting pot, but for centuries, they were not American in the true sense of the word. Blacks were, thus, not treated as descendants of people in African nations — in the way that the English and Irish and other immigrants were regarded as descendants of their people overseas. Blacks were seen as strange, inferior people whose backgrounds, languages, and culture were of absolutely no interest to white America. And this for a people whose ancestors came from the continent on which the earliest human beings appeared.

The history of African-Americans, then, has been a turbulent one. Blacks became a free people — but not necessarily an accepted people — when slavery was abolished in 1863. Up until that time, however, a black's life was about on a par with that of a farm animal. The Supreme Court's Dred Scott decision in 1857 helped see to that. Dred Scott was a slave who had been taken by his owner from Missouri, a slave state, to the northern Louisiana Purchase, a territory in which slavery was forbidden under the terms of a law called the Missouri Compromise. While there, Scott, who continued to be held as a slave, married a slave woman and they had a child. Scott and his family were later taken back to Missouri, and a few years afterward, Scott sued for freedom for himself and his family, arguing that because they had lived in a free territory, they were no longer slaves. The supreme court of Missouri ruled against Scott, saying that when he returned to the slave state he lost any freedom he may have won outside. The U.S. Supreme Court finally heard the controversial case — but it, too, ruled against Scott, arguing that under the Constitution, Negroes and their descendants could not be citizens and that Dred Scott was still a slave. The high court also ruled that the Missouri Compromise was unconstitutional because it deprived people of the right to own property, in this case, their slaves. The case triggered bitter confrontations between proslavery Americans and abolitionists — members of a radical antislavery group that began in the North — and was one of the causes of the Civil War.

One of the most famous abolitionists was Frederick Douglass (his real name was Frederick Augustus Washington Bailey), who was born a slave in Tuckahoe, Maryland, of a black mother and a white father. Taught to read by one of his owners, Douglass eventually escaped slavery and settled in New Bedford, Massachusetts. Later he edited an abolitionist newspaper and campaigned for Abraham Lincoln in the presidential election of 1860, and during the Civil War, he organized a famed regiment of black soldiers from Massachusetts. Considering Douglass's background as a slave who was cruelly treated by his masters and the fact that he was largely self-taught, his many accomplishments are remarkable. He was an eloquent orator and the "stationmaster and conductor" of the Underground Railroad, a network of people who worked secretly to smuggle slaves from the South to the North and to Canada. After the war, Douglass became the United States marshal for the District of Columbia and the U.S. minister to Haiti. An interesting sidelight to Frederick Douglass's story was that some of his opponents refused to believe he had been a slave — the fact that he could read and that he was a magnificent speaker aroused suspicions — and they put out stories that Douglass was really an impostor in the employ of the abolitionists.

Douglass worked to free the slaves through peaceful means, just as another famous African-American activist and orator, Martin Luther King, worked peacefully to gain civil rights for blacks in the 1950s and 1960s. But not all the abolitionists were nonviolent in their approach. One who eventually chose violence was a contemporary of Douglass, John Brown. Born in Torrington, Connecticut, Brown had long hated slavery, and he had one goal: to liberate the slaves in the South. In 1855, he and five of his sons went to Kansas, a hotbed of conflict between advocates of slavery and abolitionists. There, Brown fought against proslave marauders who had murdered several abolitionists. Brown and his sons killed a number of the proslavery men, and not long afterward, angrier than ever, he decided to pursue a larger goal: he would instigate an uprising among Southern slaves and free them by force. On the night of October 16, 1859, accompanied by his sons and several other abolitionists, he seized the U.S. arsenal at Harper's Ferry, Virginia, with the intention of arming the slaves and starting a rebellion. The federal government was not about to stand by and let it happen. A company of U.S. marines, commanded by Colonel Robert E. Lee, who was to oppose the North in the Civil War, retook the arsenal, killing ten of Brown's men, including two of his sons. Brown himself was wounded and captured. Charged with murder and treason, Brown was convicted and hanged in Charlestown, Virginia. Before he died, he gave a passionate speech in which he said

> I believe that to have interfered as I have done, as I have always freely admitted I have done, in behalf of God's despised poor, I did no wrong, but right. Now, if it is deemed necessary that I should forfeit my life for the furtherance of the ends of justice, and mingle my blood further with the blood of my children and with the blood of millions in this slave country whose rights are disregarded by wicked, cruel, and unjust enactments, I say, let it be done.[2]

Brown became a martyr for human rights. During the Civil War, a popular song among Northern soldiers remembered the man who had tried to right the wrong of slavery: "John Brown's body lies a-mould'ring in the grave. His soul goes marching on."

John Brown's raid further inflamed the battle between the proslavery forces and the abolitionists. A year after Brown's execution, Abraham Lincoln was elected president. The next year, 1861, the Southern states broke from the Union, and the Civil War erupted. Although there were several reasons for the war, slavery in the South was certainly one of them. A terrible price had to be paid — the loss of 600,000 lives and incalculable loss of property — but the war put an end to slavery and kept the Union intact.

Lincoln's Emancipation Proclamation, issued during the war, was a step toward freedom for the blacks. It did not actually free any slaves, but its declaration that all slaves who lived in the rebellious Southern states were "forever free" sent a strong message on how the North stood on the issue. For some time, Abraham Lincoln had merely wanted to keep the Union together; he was actually lukewarm on the issue of slavery and was willing to leave it alone where it existed. The Emancipation Proclamation represented a drastic change in Lincoln's ideas and is regarded as one of the most important pronouncements ever made by the United States. But it was actually the Thirteenth Amendment to the U.S. Constitution, adopted in 1865, that put a formal end to slavery:

> Neither slavery nor involuntary servitude, except as a punishment for a crime whereof the party shall have been duly convicted, shall exist within the United States, or any place subject to their jurisdiction. Congress shall have power to enforce this article by appropriate legislation.

It is a short piece of work, but in a few words it rights the wrong that men like Dred Scott, John Brown, and Frederick Douglass had spoken out against.

The abolition of slavery in the United States was a ray of light for human rights advocates, but it did not wipe out prejudice against blacks. Indeed, after the Civil War, bigotry was alive and thriving in the South. Although two other amendments to the Constitution, the Fourteenth and Fifteenth, were enacted, granting citizenship to former slaves and prohibiting states from denying citizens the right to vote because of race or color, bigots found many ways to get around the laws. They simply passed other laws that made blacks second-class citizens. For example, state laws said that voters had to be able to read and write, or own property, qualifications that few blacks of the day could meet. Another loophole was the so-called grandfather clause, which limited voting privileges to those men whose grandfathers had voted; since no blacks were allowed to vote before 1867, the rule effectively stopped African-Americans from exercising their right.

There were also what came to be known as Jim Crow laws. (Jim Crow was the name of a stereotyped Negro in a nineteenth-century vaudeville act.) These outrageous statutes legalized racial segregation. Blacks were not allowed to live in white areas, go to white schools, or use the same public facilities as whites; they were barred from "whites-only" restaurants and rest rooms, they could not serve on juries, and they could not ride in the front seats of buses. Any black who testified against a white person had his or her testimony thrown out of court as unreliable; marriage and sexual relations between a black man and a white woman were prohibited and punishable, but sex between a white man and a black woman, often the result of a rape, was tolerated.

Under Jim Crow, blacks had no identity outside their own shacks, for when they were at work in the cotton fields, kitchens, and factories they were, to the whites who employed them, faceless and mindless. When they were allowed to express themselves, to demonstrate that they were human, it had to be done in a way that showed they "knew their place" — no arguing with the whites, no demands, no talk about rights, just "Yes, suh" and "No, ma'am." This kind of subservience of blacks to whites came to be called Uncle Tomism. Uncle Tom, in Harriet Beecher Stowe's novel of the same name, is an old black slave cruelly treated by his overseer, Simon Legree. Tom dies as a result of a beating, and to this day blacks call blacks who bend to whites Uncle Toms.

An African-American in trouble with the law in the Jim Crow days was in trouble with more than the sheriff or the police. He had a pretty fair chance of being convicted, even if he was innocent; if he was awaiting trial, there was also a good chance he'd be dragged out of his cell and lynched; if he was lucky, he only got flogged or maybe tarred and feathered.

But an African-American didn't have to be in jail to face violence. The Ku Klux Klan saw to that. A secret white-supremacy organization formed in Tennessee after the Civil War, the KKK, with its white-sheeted Klansmen who burned crosses as a sign of their presence, harassed, lynched, and mutilated countless blacks. Later, the Klan added Catholics, Jews, and anyone involved in "un-American" activities — such as pacifism and civil rights demonstrations — to its hate list. While nowhere near as powerful as it once was, the KKK still exists, and during the turbulent 1960s, when blacks were battling for their civil rights, it carried out several attacks on civil rights workers in the South.

With the KKK as the South's unofficial policemen and upholders of racial purity, and the Jim Crow laws firmly in place, there seemed to be little that blacks could do to achieve equality, the ideal that is at the heart of the Declaration of Independence. The African-American cause was not helped at all by a Supreme Court decision in 1896, *Plessy v. Ferguson,* which ruled that a Louisiana law requiring "equal but separate accommodations for the white and colored races" on railroad cars was constitutional. This ruling established the "separate but equal" doctrine and indicated that separate facilities for blacks, such as schools, were perfectly legal, and that the states could, in effect, handle civil rights pretty much any way they pleased.

It was not until the World War II years, from 1939 to 1945, that the Jim Crow laws met any serious challenge. President Franklin D. Roosevelt ordered antidiscrimination clauses written into contracts with the federal government, and President Harry S. Truman put an end to segregation in the military. But the big blow for racial equality was struck in 1954, in yet another famous court case, one that ended in the U.S. Supreme Court. It was known as *Brown v. the Board of Education of Topeka.*

Brown represented the blacks of Topeka, Kansas, in their argument that the city's Board of Education violated the Fourteenth Amendment to the Constitution by forcing black children to go to separate and inferior schools. The Supreme Court agreed and in a historic decision, declared that the Constitution did indeed prohibit segregation in public schools. "We conclude," said the high court, "that in the field of public education the doctrine of separate but equal has no place. Separate educational facilities are inherently unequal."

While the Brown case was directed only at segregation in the public school system, its rationale easily applied to all forms of segregation under the old Jim Crow laws. A year after the Supreme Court ruling, a feisty black woman, Rosa Parks, became a symbol of the new, expanded civil rights movement when she refused to move to the back of a bus in Montgomery, Alabama. Soon, black leaders organized new political action and civil rights groups to join with the older National Association for the Advancement of Colored People (NAACP) in attempts to break down the remaining color barriers. It was not going to be an easy job. First, the school desegregation ruling had to be implemented. Although the Supreme Court had opened white schools to blacks, that was far easier said than done. In one memorable incident, the governor of Arkansas, Orval Faubus, called out National Guard troops and the state police to prevent black students from entering a high school in Little Rock. The governor's argument was that he took the strong action to prevent racial violence. President Dwight Eisenhower had to send in federal soldiers to enforce the law and allow the black students to attend classes.

Eventually, the South began desegregating its schools, and although the process was often accompanied by hostility and sometimes violence, black students and white students were sharing classrooms. Sometimes, blacks had to be taken by bus to white schools some distance from their homes, often under guard. But the school desegregation drive was at last in gear, and its success would give adult blacks the encouragement to push for segregation across the board.

Martin Luther King, Jr., a young Baptist minister from Atlanta, was one of the leaders of the movement to put an end to Jim Crow. King preached that nonviolence was the best way to achieve the blacks' goals, and he practiced what he preached. He and other black leaders organized successful bus boycotts, sit-ins, in which blacks took seats at "whites-only" lunch counters until they were waited on or arrested, and "freedom rides" to integrate bus terminals and train stations. Led by King, 200,000 African-Americans marched on Washington, D.C., in 1963 to press their demands for civil rights. There in the nation's capital, Dr. King delivered his most moving speech, in which he said

> I have a dream that one day this nation will rise up and live out the true meaning of its creed: "We hold these

> truths to be self-evident: that all men are created equal." I have a dream that one day on the red hills of Georgia the sons of former slaves and the sons of former slave-owners will be able to sit down together at the table of brotherhood.

The next year, Congress passed a Civil Rights Act that banned discrimination against blacks in public accommodations, labor unions, and employment. In 1965, another historic law was passed, the Voting Rights Act, which guaranteed blacks their right to vote; three years later, another bill banning discrimination was passed.

Recounting the victories in this way, however, makes it appear that the gains were made easily, and that they were the solutions to all the blacks' problems. They were neither. The African-Americans' cause had the backing of leaders such as Presidents John F. Kennedy and Lyndon B. Johnson, but even support on a national level did not stop opponents of desegregation. And sometimes, the nonviolent protests that blacks believed in were not always met with nonviolent arguments: club-wielding police were often called out to beat the demonstrators, dogs were set on them, fire hoses and tear gas were turned on them, and sometimes, fatal shots were fired. The homes of black leaders were bombed, and in one despicable demonstration of how deep racism runs, four African-American children were killed when a bomb exploded in a church during a Sunday School class. Terrible, too, was the assassination in 1968 of Dr. King, who four years earlier had been awarded the Nobel Peace Prize.

The violent acts directed against blacks served only to turn much of the nation against the pro-segregation forces and fuel the courage and determination of African-Americans — such as the woman who refused to answer a judge who had called her by her first name until she was addressed as Miss, as he would have addressed a white woman. One cannot help but admire the persistent struggle for freedom by blacks and their leaders, both black and white. As Lyndon Johnson put it in a moving speech on the voting rights bill and on civil rights:

> The time for justice has come. No force can hold it back. It is right — in the eyes of man and God — that it should

> come. And when it does, that day will brighten the lives of every American.[3]

Then Johnson slowly repeated the words of the song that had become the anthem of the civil rights movement: "We shall overcome."

True to the promise of those lyrics, blacks have overcome a lot; today they are represented in just about every profession and endeavor that whites are — from sports to the arts and sciences, to politics and business, to religion and the law. A recent study by the Population Reference Bureau found that one out of seven black families earns $50,000 or more, compared to one out of seventeen black families who made that much money some twenty-five years ago. Blacks have exerted a good deal of influence over life in America, and it sometimes came even during the Jim Crow days — in 1947, Jackie Robinson broke through the color barrier when he became the first black to play baseball in the major leagues. Ralph Bunche, an extraordinary black statesman, won the Nobel Peace Prize in 1950 for mediating the dispute between the Arabs and the Palestinians — at a time when Jim Crow would have kept him from eating in a white restaurant in the South. In science, George Washington Carver, born to slave parents, became the first black scientist to make a national reputation — ironically helping the economy of the South by developing hundreds of uses for peanuts and sweet potatoes. And on the U.S. Supreme Court, there was Thurgood Marshall, great-grandson of a slave and the first black justice on the high court, the man who argued the *Brown v. Board of Education* case before that very court when he was chief counsel for the NAACP.

Much of the progress African-Americans achieved came through determination, willingness to work within the system, repressive as it was, and nonviolent protest. Other times, militancy and violence were seen as a way to get the job done. Fueled by the murder of Dr. King and the belief of many of the militants that change was coming too slow, the style of the civil rights movement changed drastically in the late 1960s. Radical groups such as the Black Panthers sprang up to beat the drum for revolution among blacks as the only way to achieve racial equality. Riots broke out in many American cities. In the black Watts section of Los Angeles, more than thirty people died in clashes with police. "Violence is necessary," said one black militant, H. Rap Brown. "It is as American as cherry pie." Black Power became a rallying cry for those who took pride in African-American culture and achievement. Malcolm X, an outspoken Black Muslim, exhorted blacks to separate from whites; he later changed his views, suggesting that the two groups might live together, and was assassinated by blacks.

During those turbulent years, militant blacks chided other blacks for being to complacent, calling them Uncle Toms, snowflakes, or Oreo cookies if they gave in to whites. A hero of the time was W. E. B. Du Bois, the radical black writer and teacher who helped found the NAACP. Du Bois, who died in 1963, was a member of the American Communist Party. Among his favorite targets was Booker T. Washington, an American educator who was born of a black slave woman and a white man on a Virginia plantation and who championed educational and economic gains for blacks. Washington founded Tuskegee Institute in Alabama, transforming it from a shack into a collection of more than forty buildings. First educated in night school, Washington received an honorary degree from Harvard University in 1896. But while Washington was in favor of education for blacks, he argued that they should not concentrate on achieving political and social equality but should, rather, accommodate whites. Black leaders like Du Bois found this view offensive and regarded him as the white man's token Negro. Still, some of Washington's addresses bear hearing today for their hopeful tone:

"In working out our destiny," he said in a speech after he received his Harvard honor,

> While the main burden and center of activity must be with us, we shall need in a large measure in the years that are to come as we have in the past, the help, the encouragement, the guidance that the strong can give the weak. Thus helped, we of both races in the South soon shall throw off the shackles of racial and sectional prejudices and rise . . . above the clouds of ignorance, narrowness, and selfishness, into that atmosphere, that pure sunshine, where it will be our highest ambition to serve man, our brother, regardless of race or previous condition.[4]

Despite the bright promises and all that African-Americans achieved, there is still a great deal left for them to overcome. The roots of inequality still run deep, and far too many whites are still wary of or hostile to blacks. For every great black poet such as Langston Hughes, there are countless blacks who still cannot read and write. For every successful black film director such as Spike Lee, there are many, many blacks who cannot afford the price of a movie. For every Michael Jordan, there are young African-American basketball players who will never be discovered because the only courts they'll ever play on will not be in high school or college but in a vacant lot hidden in the shadow of rundown tenements. For every Clarence Thomas, there are too many blacks standing on the other side of the judge's bench or crowding our prisons. For every black who marries a white, there are far more whites who are appalled by such a relationship. For every judicial decision or new law that adds to civil rights for African-Americans, another judicial decision or new law takes away the gain. For every black who moves into a "whites-only" neighborhood, there is the possibility of having his or her house burned down. For every black who has white friends, there are blacks jeered, blocked from visiting a white neighborhood, and sometimes beaten to death there. Black is beautiful, a popular black pride slogan tells us. But for those who shout "White Power!" and "Go back to Africa!" black is still ugly, something to be shunned.

If any doubt remains that blacks are still not treated equally with whites, and sometimes are even shut out of society, consider the following:

- While more American blacks are affluent today, the total worth of all their assets, that is, their wealth, is far less than the net worth of affluent whites.
- Blacks are only half as likely to go to college as whites, and those with degrees make one-third less income than do whites with the same education.[5]
- The poverty rate among blacks has been about three times that of whites for the past twenty years, and black infants are twice as likely to die of illness as are white babies.
- Although blacks comprise about 12 percent of the U.S.

population and more than 11 percent of all magazine readers, they appear in only 4.5 percent of magazine advertisements; when blacks do appear, they are usually portrayed as athletes, musicians, or objects of charity.[6]

- When blacks shop, they are more apt to be watched by security guards, and more at risk of being questioned, searched, and accused. "Blacks are seen as shoplifters, as unclean, as disreputable poor," said sociologist Joe R. Feagin of the University of Florida. "No matter how affluent and influential, a black person cannot escape the stigma of being black even while relaxing or shopping."[7]
- Although the practice is illegal, some clubs still charge blacks higher membership rates, give them fewer benefits, and deny them financing.
- Several police departments around the country — Los Angeles and New York City among them — have recently come under fire for mistreating black suspects, a situation that forced the U.S. Justice Department to review some 15,000 cases over the last few years to determine if there has been a pattern of police brutality against minorities. In one of the most widely publicized cases of 1992, Rodney King, a black motorist who had been stopped by police in Los Angeles, was severely beaten by the officers; a witness's videotape of the assault led to an investigation of the police department. The officer in charge was accused of failing to stop his men from using unnecessary force, of failing to open an investigation into the incident, and of failing to file an accurate report. Another policeman was accused of hitting the motorist repeatedly with his stick and of making racial slurs over a mobile police computer; still another was seen on the tape kicking the helpless motorist.

The policemen went on trial for beating Rodney King, and the brutal videotape was played for the jury. The attorneys for the accused policemen argued that King had not been badly hurt, that he was dangerous, and that the officers believed he was going to attack them as they tried to arrest him. The prosecution pointed to the videotape's apparent evidence of police brutality, and one of the officers testified that the others were out of control on the night of the beating, and that he had tried to restrain them. Despite the videotaped evidence, which many people believed was proof that the policemen were guilty, the jurors acquitted the officers.

The verdict touched off the worst urban riots in United States history. The depressed South Central area of Los Angeles was burned and looted by gangs of angry blacks who also attacked whites in the neighborhood.

(At this writing, a federal grand jury has indicted the officers for violating King's civil rights.)

- In 1991, a special commission on minorities charged that New York state's court system was "infested with racism," that members of minority groups were less likely than whites to serve on juries, that blacks received less favorable action when they were plaintiffs, and that minority lawyers experienced racial bias, including jokes and stereotyping by opposing lawyers. One judge was quoted as saying from the bench, "There's another nigger in the woodpile."[8]
- Civil rights groups have recently accused courts in some states (Georgia, which leads the nation in executions, is among them) of seeking the death penalty more often when a black kills a white than when the crime is the other way around. Said George Kendall, a lawyer for the NAACP, "It's the race of victims that drives this thing. The tradition of the black codes and the slave codes, which provided different, harsher punishments for offenders who harmed whites than blacks, remains today."[9]
- Some thirty years years after the first black enrolled at the University of Mississippi, the U.S. Supreme Court, in 1991, finally agreed to determine whether segregation still lives on in the state's colleges and whether the

civil rights laws apply to higher education as well as to public elementary and secondary schools. Students in the state's five traditionally white colleges are still mostly white, and in the three traditionally black colleges, black.

- In 1987, forty years after Jackie Robinson broke baseball's color barrier, a vice president of the Los Angeles Dodgers remarked that blacks may not have "some of the necessities" that would allow them to hold management positions in professional baseball. He was dismissed, but the remark was not forgotten. Hank Aaron, the home run star who is a vice president of the Atlanta Braves, commented, "No one talks about it anymore, but it's still the same situation: two black managers, no black general managers, hardly any doctors and lawyers affiliated with baseball on the major and minor league levels, and very few attempts to use black-owned companies for various services. You have teams changing managers all the time, and you don't see any blacks."[10]

Discrimination against blacks is not confined to the United States, either. Countries that flooded the U.S. with immigrants in the 1800s and 1900s are themselves treating immigrants, many of them black, shabbily. In Milan and Florence, Italian cities known for fashion and culture respectively, protests and violent attacks directed against Africans are increasing; in Berlin, new Nazis warn against mixing races and beat up Africans. Closer to home, in Québec, Canada, police shot and killed an unarmed black father of two, contributing to mounting racial tensions. But perhaps the most glaring example of all outside the United States comes from South Africa, where apartheid has forced blacks to live separately from whites for many years. In a historic move, most of the discriminatory laws were scrapped recently, including one that defined all South Africans by race. That law governed who could use public facilities such as toilets, swimming pools, and parks. The government even employed "race detectives" to determine who was black. Here's how one journalist describes the process:

> The tests . . . used to determine race in the myriad "borderline" cases would be worthy of a Monty Python farce if the consequences were not so tragic. They included shoving a pencil into curly hair and making the subject shake his or her head. If the pencil stuck, the person was pronounced black; if it dislodged, the person was considered "coloured" on the assumption that coloured hair is less tightly crimped than black hair.
>
> The shapes of buttocks and jaw lines were inspected, and people were pinched to see if they exclaimed in Afrikaans, the language of the white and coloured rather than the black person, or said "ouch!" in an African tongue. Unmarried mothers who could not produce an identity card of a child's father when they registered its birth were often made to undress the child so that the "race inspector" could look for the telltale "Mongolian blue spot" — dark patches over the sacrum which supposedly indicated coloured blood and earned babies the nickname "blue bums."[11]

Fortunately, this sort of testing is over now. But armed men, members of pro-apartheid groups, still harass blacks in South Africa. And black leaders, while they welcome the changes, argue that there is still much to be done before all traces of apartheid are wiped out and that the government has not done as much as it could to stop the violence still directed against blacks.

Is it any wonder, in light of all this, that many blacks push so hard for attention? Isn't it understandable why some black high school students hold separate senior proms? Why some young black men swagger and commit crimes against whites? Why some black historians have been saying that Africans sailed to the Americas way before Columbus? Why blacks, along with other minorities that have been denied opportunity, sometimes demand what often appears to be special treatment? If whites were constantly put down, were looked on with suspicion every time they walked into a supermarket or department store, were cut out of jobs because of their race, or were regarded as subhuman, they would not like it, either.

The fact is, integration is still not complete, and prejudice against blacks is still a fact of life. Yes, a bagful of laws proclaims the rights of blacks and tells whites how to behave toward blacks. More laws are being written; more landmark cases are being heard. White supremacist leaders have been successfully prosecuted and their organizations bankrupted — in one case the mother of a lynched black youth was, ironically, awarded the deed to the anti-black organization's national headquarters. College faculty committees rebuke teachers for making racist remarks and sometimes even dismiss them; the FBI, facing charges that white agents harassed a black agent, considers disciplining the offenders; radio stations would think twice today about playing old recordings of *The Amos 'n' Andy Show,* a popular series some years ago about the wheeling and dealing of two "shiftless" southern black men (they were actually played by whites) who traveled north to seek their fortune; the minstrel show, in which white actors painted their faces black, strummed banjos, and sang and spoke in exaggerated black dialogue, is long gone, along with other black stereotypes that were popular in less caring times.

The laws and the courts and public opinion have helped the African-American cause, of course, and our country is a better place for some blacks — and the *some* has to be emphasized — than it was in the 1960s. But are the changes that have come enough? The answer is no. Stereotypes still exist, some of them the legacy of the minstrel shows, the *Amos 'n' Andy* broadcasts, and that box with Aunt Jemima's picture on the front. There are the racist jokes about blacks, the insult in the watermelon a white racist holds over his head when blacks march into "his" neighborhood.

Many people feel that establishing quotas for blacks in jobs, preferential treatment in hiring, and "race norming" — the practice of adjusting scores on job-placement exams to make blacks and other minorities look better on paper — are the ways to help African-Americans overcome the stereotypes. Programs that require employers to place more blacks and other minorities in jobs that have gone to whites for many years are part of a federal policy called Affirmative Action. Affirmative Action remains controversial even though it has been around for many years. Its backers say that it is the only way to get integration on track, that it is the only fair thing to do in light of the discrimination of past years. Critics argue that Affirmative Action is a reverse form of discrimination, that it favors a less qualified person over a qualified one. That issue was the subject of yet another Supreme Court case, in 1978. The plaintiff was Allan Bakke, a white man who had been refused admission to a medical school that had accepted black applicants even though their academic qualifications were weaker than his. The high court decided that Bakke had indeed been illegally denied acceptance but that medical schools did have the right to consider race when they admitted students.

Both sides in the Affirmative Action debate make good arguments, just as do both sides in the debates over abortion and capital punishment. But it is difficult to keep personal feelings out of the positions people take. Those who favor Affirmative Action sometimes charge that opponents are not really interested in fair treatment but only in keeping African-Americans and other minorities down. Those who oppose it say advancement in any profession ought to be based only on merit and that those who favor Affirmative Action just want a free ride.

It is true that sometimes people need a boost, a way to cut through unnecessary red tape to get a job, an introduction. There really is nothing wrong with that, especially if the person has been cut out because of skin color and provided the person trying to get in is not going in over his or her head. But putting someone in a job *only* because he or she is black or white, with little thought given to whether they are qualified, is risky. The person may not be able to handle the job and may then do it poorly and hurt his or her chances for future employment; moreover, people in over their heads may produce shoddy products or provide unsatisfactory service, which translates into loss of profit for the company.

Unfair as it is, it is clear that African-Americans and other minorities still must struggle to get the things that some people manage to get without even trying. This does not mean that whites should stop helping blacks. They have to help — through their support of legislation that corrects obvious wrongs, by emphasizing the necessity for education and providing the means for it, by appreciating that blacks have a history and a culture, by extending a friendly hand, sometimes even an extra one.

Helping does not mean, however, that blacks should be led around by people who may know more than they or are more privileged than they — this was the attitude held by the colonial governments all over the world who took care of their "little brown brothers" and by the architects of apartheid. Helping means assisting, which, according to an old French proverb, is the law of nature. One of the best ways to assist is to help people help themselves. Clarence Thomas, the African-American lawyer and judge whose nomination to the U.S. Supreme Court by President Bush was opposed by many African-Americans because Thomas's views on racial matters seemed too conservative, once expressed the ideal of self-reliance this way:

> I was raised to survive under the totalitarianism of segregation, not only without the active assistance of government but with its active opposition. We were raised to survive in spite of the dark oppressive cloud of governmentally sanctioned bigotry. Self-sufficiency and spiritual and emotional security were our tools to carve out and secure freedom. Those who attempt to capture the daily counseling, oversight, common sense, and vision of my grandparents in a governmental program are engaging in sheer folly. Government cannot develop individual responsibility, but it certainly can refrain from preventing or hindering the development of this responsibility.[12]

It really makes no difference whether Thomas agrees with other African-Americans on how racial equality is achieved. There are many approaches. What is important is that the gap between whites and blacks be narrowed, if not eliminated. New York City's African-American mayor, David Dinkins, put it eloquently, and though his advice may seem obvious, it is sound, for it is the only way to achieve racial harmony:

> As frustrations build and pressures mount, people are more likely to lash out. In tough times, child abuse increases, alcohol abuse rises, and the bonds of civility and decency fray.
>
> Unfortunately, some small-minded people prey upon these pressures, spreading a message not of unity but of

division, and fixing the blame not on the social and economic challenges we share but on those who are alien and different.

I challenge all of the people of this city to reject these calls to bigotry, because if the bigots succeed in spreading their poison, it's nobody's fault but our own.

Right now, each of you must look into your own hearts, in your own families. Look honestly at yourselves — and your own communities — and ask whether you can be swayed by prejudice, and what you're going to do about it. Because no matter how much government can do, government cannot substitute for the content of our character.[13]

3 • RELIGIOUS PREJUDICE
Hatred in the Name of God

O unbelievers, I will not worship that which ye worship; nor will ye worship that which I worship. Ye have your religion, and I have my religion.
— The Koran

Religion is the sign of the hard-pressed creature, the heart of a heartless world, as it is the soul of soulless circumstances. It is the opium of the people.
— Karl Marx

Half of the world's people believe in a single God, while many others, like the Hindus, worship many different ones. The wide difference of opinion over which God or gods really warrant our attention often causes people of different religious faiths to be at odds, sometimes violently so.

Which seems strange, considering that religion is about loving one's neighbor, about mercy and charity and justice, and finding the right way to lead a decent life. Religion helps us fight pain, lessen anxiety, and deal with all of the other obstacles we encounter throughout our lives. But while religion is, as someone once said, a wise man's foundation, it is also a bigot's tool. Bigots often use religion as a way to judge other people. They punish people whose religion runs counter to their own by depriving them of a job or political office, they go to war with countries because their religious orientation is perceived as a threat, and they upset the lives of primitive peoples, whose "savage" beliefs are not mainstream faiths, by trying to convert them.

Religion, thus, has been at the root of much conflict between people of different cultures for centuries. Human beings have always worshiped some higher being, but they have also argued about which being is highest. Indeed, wars are still fought over religion today.

No one can prove which religion is the "right" one, but that does not stop some people from mocking another religion that they regard as false or foolish or threatening.

Many religious individuals respect the faith of others and do not feel any need to force others to believe as they do. And while it's been said that the more devout a person is, the more authoritarian he or she may be and the less apt to be tolerant of others' beliefs, there are many fervent believers who are simply happy going their own way, confident in the knowledge that their road will lead them to salvation. They may believe that if others do not follow that road, they will still get there in their own way. Others — and the devout, unfortunately, can be among them — feel that because theirs is without any doubt the one and true religion, it is their right and duty to bring others to their side. The "nonbelievers" have lost their way and can be saved only if they embrace the "true faith."

It is not my purpose to place one particular religion on the side of angels but to show that all religions have a right to exist and their followers the right to be treated with dignity and respect. Unfortunately, this has not been the case throughout history.

Whatever it is that makes a person a religious bigot — and usually the reason has less to do with religious training than with other deep-rooted prejudices and insecurities and with the need to wield power — religious intolerance is as harmful as any other kind. Let's examine some of the notable instances of religious bigotry and the problems each created.

Ancient Rome is a good place to begin. The Romans worshiped a huge family of gods, all of them borrowed from the Greeks. There were, among many others, Apollo, god of the sun; Mars, god of war; Neptune, god of the ocean; and Jupiter, the king of them all. With such a collection of deities to rule over the earth, the waters, the sky, and a host of other regions, as well as over phenomena such as war, wisdom, and fertility, it must have been quite irritating to the Romans when they heard of the one God that the Jews and the Christians worshiped. The Jews (whose experiences we'll discuss in more detail in the next chapter) felt the wrath of the Romans when Jerusalem was destroyed; when Roman legions attacked them at a great rock called Masada in the Judaean desert, forcing the defenders, a fiercely dedicated group of Jews known as Zealots, to commit suicide en masse rather than surrender; and when Jesus of Nazareth, a Jew, was sentenced to death by the Roman governor.

The Christians bore the brunt of Roman religious persecution during the reign of the Emperor Nero, who accused them of causing a huge fire that destroyed Rome. Nero had his own reasons for blaming the Christians for the fire, and they went beyond intolerance of their religion. Nero merely used the Christian religion as an excuse to divert attention from his own crimes: he had killed members of his own family, and people were suspicious that it was he who had started the great fire. Roman emperors were venerated as gods, and some people actually worshiped the emperor. So when Christians started praying to another God, hatred for the sect grew. Many Romans also believed that because the Christians taught that the bread and wine they drank at their ceremonies were actually the body and blood of Christ, that meant that the Christians were really cannibals. There were stories that the Christians murdered and ate children as part of their rituals. It was, therefore, easy for Nero to take advantage of the popular myths about the Christians. And so when he started executing Christians in public in the Great Circus in Rome, sometimes feeding them to wild animals, he had enormous support from the citizens.

Later, it was illegal to be a Christian in Rome, and anyone who admitted to it was executed. The only way a Christian could be spared was to renounce his or her faith and worship the Roman gods. Because so many Christians were being persecuted, several of their leaders, known as apologists, began speaking out in defense of the faith. One of the most outspoken apologists was Saint Justin the Philosopher, who was born about 100 A.D. He had been a pagan, someone who believed in the ancient gods or no gods or God at all, but when he was about thirty years old, he devoted himself to Christian teachings. Justin opened a school of philosophy in Rome, and after winning one heated debate with a Cynic — a believer in the philosophical teaching that stressed independence — he was exposed by his opponent as a Christian. Justin was put on trial, and even though he wrote an impassioned letter to the emperor, Antoninus, in which he defended Christian thinking, he was tortured. When he refused to pay homage to the Roman gods, he was beheaded, suffering a martyr's death.

Despite the persecutions, however, many Romans began to be impressed by the unselfishness and the generosity of the Christians, who were quite poor but still seemed to have a deep sympathy for people worse off than they. An increasing number of Romans joined the Christians, and soon the Christian church was a powerful organization in the Roman Empire. Eventually, the Roman emperor Constantine the Great became one himself and made Christianity the official state religion.

Christianity's central power was now located in Rome, and the bishops of that city, the popes, were regarded in western Europe as rulers of the whole church. But the stage had been set for more tumult in the Christian world. The eastern part of the Roman empire, made up of parts of Europe and Asia, with its capital in the ancient Greek city of Constantinople, was beginning to expand. It would be known as the Byzantine Empire with its own emperor and its own religion, an offshoot of Christianity called the Eastern Orthodox church.

Relations between the churches of the East and West were strained. Each empire had its own views of how much influence the church and the emperor should have, which articles of faith were most important, which traditions would be followed or scrapped. In the end, the differences of opinion were so great that the Roman church broke off with the Eastern churches, and the schism never fully healed.

There followed other breaks within the Christian church, divisions that sowed the seeds of prejudice among Christians; and there were breaks between Christianity and the various other religions of the East, which created tremendous and long-lasting animosity on both sides. Moreover, the differences were not all expressed nonviolently: massacres and wars underscored just how deep the bitterness ran.

Perhaps the best-known holy wars, if one can use such a seemingly contradictory phrase when referring to battles over religious differences, were the Crusades. These were a bloody series of wars undertaken by European Christians between the eleventh and thirteenth centuries to retake the Holy Land — the territory where Jesus had lived — from the Muslims. The Muslims (or Moslems) were followers of Mohammed, the founder of Islam and prophet of "the only god," Allah.

Angered over the Arabs' occupation of holy territory and bent on revenge for the persecution of Christians living in the area, two wandering, fanatical preachers, Peter the Hermit and Walter the Penniless, roused the crusading spirit all over Europe in 1095 A.D. While Peter was visiting Jerusalem, so the story goes, he was appalled by the treatment of Christians and pilgrims at the hands of the infidels, as the Muslims were known by the Christians. In a temple, he heard what he believed to be the voice of God telling him, "Rise, Peter, go forth to make known the tribulations of my people. The hour is come for the delivery of my servants, for the recovery of the Holy Places."

Peter returned to Europe and supposedly brought his divine instructions to Pope Urban II, who sanctioned the First Crusade. It had a beginning that Christians would like to forget. Before formal plans could be made to raise a properly trained army, Peter and his cohorts raised a huge army of rabble on their own and marched toward Constantinople, slaughtering Jews and plundering villages in Hungary and Bulgaria along the way. By the time the undisciplined "soldiers" got to Constantinople, they were thoroughly disorganized. Trapped and overwhelmed by the far superior Muslims, the ragtag troops were destroyed. Peter managed to get away, and when a formal army of 200,000 well-trained Crusaders was finally sent to the East, he joined it and shared in the victory over Jerusalem — despite the fact that he had deserted his men earlier.

The First Crusade was the only successful one. It captured Jerusalem and established a Christian kingdom in Palestine. It enhanced the power of the pope and widened the church's domain. In the minds of the Crusaders, all of that justified the waging of a "religious" war. But the Crusaders were not all that holy, despite the crimson crosses emblazoned on their shields and

tend to seek only the glory of God," wrote the British philosopher Herbert Spencer, "but if there were a window to look into their hearts, we would find nothing there but self-seeking."

A few Europeans probably did learn something from the bloody experience of the Crusades. The veterans learned that the Muslim Knights of the Crescent were brave and formidable opponents, not simply a pack of fanatics. The Christian soldiers would never forget the chivalry of Saladin, the Muslim military leader and sultan who retook Jerusalem and then allowed Christians access to it. The Crusades also familiarized Europeans with the goods and customs of the East and made them realize that Europe was not the only place on earth that appreciated beauty and richness of thought. As the historian Hendrik Van Loon wrote many years ago:

> Of course, it would never do to say this openly. But when the Crusader returned home, he was likely to imitate the manners which he had learned from his heathenish foe, compared to whom the average western knight was still a good deal of a country bumpkin. He also brought with him several new foodstuffs, such as peaches and spinach, which he planted in his garden and grew for his own benefit. He gave up the barbarous custom of wearing a load of heavy armour and appeared in the flowing robes of silk or cotton which were the traditional habit of the followers of the Prophet and were originally worn by the Turks. Indeed the Crusades, which had begun as a punitive expedition against the Heathen, became a course of general instruction in civilisation for millions of young Europeans.[2]

Unfortunately, the positive lessons of the Crusades had little effect on future relations between Christians and Muslims. They continued to battle one another, and the Muslims generally got the worst of it. Over the centuries, Muslim influence was halted by the Dutch in Indonesia, by the British in India and Egypt, by the French in Algeria and Morocco, by the Spanish in Granada, and by the Allied powers who dismantled the Ottoman Empire of the Turks during World War I. With such a long history of war-

tunics. When they took Jerusalem in 1099, they butchered Je along with the Muslims. During the Second Crusade, the Chi tian armies robbed, massacred, and raped their way across B antine lands, apparently taking to heart the war cry of its mo vocal advocate, Saint Bernard of France:

> Fly then to arms. Let a holy rage animate you in the figh and let the Christian world resound with these words the prophet, "Cursed be he who does not stain his swor with blood!"[1]

In the Fourth Crusade, perhaps the most self-serving of the wars the Christian armies took advantage of their battle with the Mus lims to conquer the Byzantine Empire and the Eastern Orthodox Church, something the leaders of the Eastern empire had long suspected was coming. Latin religious leaders were put in charge of the East's churches, and the Latin Empire of Constantinople was born. The hatred that resulted further divided the Christian churches, and only today have steps been taken to try to reconcile the Roman and Orthodox faiths.

In the final analysis, the Crusades were a failure. Jerusalem didn't remain in Christian hands for long, and the Arabs soon took back all the land they had lost earlier. The First Crusade might have benefited the Roman church, but it and the subsequent campaigns probably did much to build hatred among various religious groups, hatred that stands to this day. The Crusades were, for all their glorious aims, a hypocrisy. The Crusaders considered their Muslim enemies heathens, but in reality the Muslims were not unlike Christians in that they followed a daughter religion of Judaism. Islam honors Jewish and Christian prophets, including Jesus, and it is based on the belief in one God. Some Muslims may be fanatical in their belief — to the extent that they will try to wipe out all other beliefs and even die in that cause — but one could say the same for many Christians, especially those who directed and fought in the Crusades. There was religious frenzy on both sides of the wars of the Crusades, but there was also the quest for power and influence, for more land for the respective empires. "Thus there are many in this world who pre-

fare and hatred behind them, it is easy to see why even today Christians and Muslims view each other with suspicion.

The Muslims who have held Western hostages in Lebanon were not motivated by religious reasons but by political ones. Neither were the Allied forces (most of whom were Christians) who bombed Baghdad during the Gulf War doing it because it was a war between Christians and Muslims. And yet in the minds of many Christians and Muslims, these events were further proof of the division between people of two faiths. Given the past, it is easy for some Christians to blame Islam for the hostage taking and argue that it only confirms what some Christians have long felt about the followers of Mohammed, that they are all terrorists and fanatics. Muslims may just as easily wonder whether the attacks on Iraq were just one more in the long series of Christian assaults against Arabs, one more attempt to conquer yet another Arab stronghold.

Some Muslims are terrorists, and centuries ago, Mohammed massacred many Jews because they would not accept his claim to be the greater prophet promised by Moses. And, by the same token, some Christian leaders would like nothing better than to see Arab states humiliated and Islam dead. But to draw from these realities that all Muslims are to be feared and hated is wrong and leads to irrational prejudice. And unfortunately, many people have negative feelings about Islam and its followers, if they have any feelings at all about one of the world's three great "one-God" religions. If you are a Christian or a Jew, how many Muslims do you actually know? You know many members of each other's faiths, and you probably know something about their religion. But what do you know about Muslims beyond that some have caused a lot of problems for America and its interests in the Middle East or that the Crusaders fought against them hundreds of years ago or that some Muslim women wear veils?

You're not alone if you know little or nothing about Muslims beyond what you read in the papers or saw on television every time a new hostage deal was announced, or when Arab terrorists hijacked a jetliner, or when a new death threat was issued against Salman Rushdie, the novelist who wrote *The Satanic Verses,* a book many Muslims felt was blasphemous. Perhaps that narrow view of

Islam is why some polls showed that hostility toward Arabs was at a record level in 1990 in the United States. Iraq's invasion of Kuwait obviously played a part in the increase of anti-Arab sentiment, which included everything from threatening telephone calls to Arab-Americans to arson. But ignorance of a whole group of people was also to blame. "It is as though Arabs are put into one bag and shaken up and one is picked out to be targeted," said the president of the American-Arab Anti-Discrimination Committee.[3] Once again, individuals are blamed for something they had nothing to do with, blamed because they happen to belong to a certain group of people.

Such intolerance is not always just a matter of Christians versus Muslim or Muslims versus Jews. Within religions themselves there is often deep hostility toward one branch or another, and over history this hostility has sometimes turned violent. One example is the division within Islam between the Sunni Muslims and the Shiite Muslims. When Mohammed died in 632, the Sunnis accepted the authority of the caliphs, or rulers, who succeeded him. But the Shiites argued that only Mohammed's relatives could be rulers, and they wanted the prophet's son-in-law, Ali, to be the new leader of the Muslims. Ali did eventually serve as caliph, until he was murdered in 661. The Shiites then said that his son Hussein must become the leader, but the caliphate was seized by the governor of Syria. The Shiites fought unsuccessfully to challenge the new caliph's rule. Hussein was killed in battle, and the ruling power passed away from the line of Mohammed's descendants. Ever since, the Shiites have felt that they are governed wrongly, and bloody confrontations between the two groups are commonplace today. Shiites are generally treated shabbily in Arab countries — except in Iran, where they are a majority of the population — and are prevented from holding important government positions. A harsh price to pay for a religious difference of opinion that occurred more than 1,300 years ago, but one that demonstrates quite clearly just how long-lasting, and irrational, prejudice is.

Another split, within Roman Catholicism, occurred much more recently than the rift among Muslims, and although it has not resulted in the suffering and maltreatment the Muslim schism caused, it set the stage for religious prejudices that exist to this day. The split was the Reformation, the religious reform movement that began as an effort to change the Roman Catholic church but resulted in the establishment of the Protestant churches. The first signs of the movement came in the 1300s with the speeches and writings of the English theologian John Wycliffe, who was known as the Morning Star of the Reformation. Wycliffe bravely attacked the Catholic church's time-honored teachings, but he learned soon enough that taking on the pope was a hard game. The Vatican did all it could to silence Wycliffe. He was condemned by Rome, his writings were suppressed, and he was ordered imprisoned. But Wycliffe continued to preach and write against papal authority until he died. Even then, the church would not let him rest: Wycliffe's bones were dug out of his grave and burned, and the ashes thrown into a river. Even worse was the punishment the church handed out to Wycliffe's followers. John Huss, a Czech Catholic priest, was one who fared badly: he was excommunicated and burned at the stake for spreading Wycliffe's words.

Years later, Martin Luther, the renowned bible translator and former Catholic monk, led a full-scale Reformation in Germany. In 1517, he published a scathing attack against the Catholic church's sale of indulgences, which were pardons from punishment for sin that the church granted when the sinner recited certain prayers. Condemned as a heretic by his church, Luther was threatened with excommunication by the pope — to which he responded by publicly burning the pope's letter and by renouncing all allegiance to the papacy. He was then formally excommunicated. "I neither can nor will retract anything," he said in his most famous defense of his views, "for it cannot be right for a Christian to speak against his conscience. I stand here and can say no more. God help me. Amen."

The Reformation spread throughout Europe, and when it reached England, King Henry VIII was one of those who welcomed it. Henry wanted to divorce Catherine of Aragon and marry Anne Boleyn, and when the pope refused to give him permission, Henry went ahead anyway. Henry eventually declared himself, not the pope, head of the Christian church in England, which came to be known as the Church of England.

The Reformation grew out of a peaceful movement to abolish

Catholic practices that many religious leaders felt were either scripturally wrong or corrupt. It too, however, had its violent side. A number of religious wars were fought during the turbulent period, among them the Thirty Years' War, which raged from 1618 to 1648 in central Europe. This long, savage struggle for religious, territorial, and political power pitted Catholics against Protestants, and when it was finally over, millions were dead and whole countries were in ruins. Germany, where most of the war was waged, suffered enormously: its population was said to have been reduced from 15 million to 5 million people.

Peace was restored eventually, and many countries became stronger than they had been before. France became the dominant power, but the authority of the Holy Roman Empire was severely diminished; individual leaders, not some central authority, dictated the religion each country would follow. Some countries remained Catholic, others Protestant, or strict followers of one Protestant sect.

Historians say that the peace that followed the Thirty Years' War made Catholics and Protestants equally tolerant of one another because each religion had carved out its own spheres of influence. But although the conflict was the last major war between Protestants and Catholics, the old hatreds and suspicions that members of each faith directed against each other never died. Born of ignorance and spread by bigots, these negative feelings have stayed with us down through the centuries.

For years, Catholics and Protestants in British-controlled Northern Ireland have been at odds, with people on both sides resorting to violence. While territorial and political goals are the main issue — Catholic nationalists in the south and many Catholics in the North want to see a united Ireland free of British control — the friction between the two Christian religions is always there.

Catholics and Protestants are not the only ones who battle each other. In Nigeria, armed clashes erupt regularly between the Muslim majority and the Christian minority. Relations between the two groups are so tense that the government does not dare ask people to disclose their religion when the census is taken. In Yugoslavia, Orthodox Serbs and Catholic Croats have been engaged in bloody confrontations ever since the countries of eastern Europe gained their independence.

Fortunately, one's religion in the United States does not often put a person at as grave risk as in Northern Ireland, Nigeria, or Yugoslavia, but it can sometimes be a hindrance. In 1928, Alfred Smith, the Democratic governor of New York, became the first Catholic to be nominated for president of the United States. He was beaten badly in the election by the Republican candidate, Herbert Hoover — and chief among the reasons for his defeat was the belief of many Protestants that as a Catholic, Smith could never free himself from the authority of the pope. It was not until 1960, when John F. Kennedy was elected the first Catholic president, that some of the old fears were put to rest. Kennedy was able to convince Protestant voters that he believed strongly in the separation of church and state and that he would follow his conscience and the national interest when he made decisions and not be swayed by any divine power or threat of punishment.

But convincing members of another faith that yours is not a threat can be a very difficult task, again because myths, misconceptions, and suspicions are so firmly rooted. The job becomes even more difficult when you're in the minority. The majority too often takes to heart the idea that it rules and that a minority has no rights. This narrow view has done grave disservice to many religions in the United States over the years, not so much to the mainstream Protestant and Catholic religions but to those that sprang up with sets of beliefs and rituals that ran counter to conventional Christian beliefs.

Two that have suffered greatly come to mind: Quakers and Mormons. At one time in America, members of these sects were severely persecuted and sometimes killed by fellow Christians who disagreed with their teachings.

First we'll look at the Quakers, whose real name is the Religious Society of Friends. Organized in England in 1647, the Friends refused to accept standard Protestant teachings and rules, including the need for scripture and priests; they refused to pay tithes (the traditional tenth of one's income that went to support the church), to take oaths, and to bear arms. Instead, they focused on a belief in the "inner light," the presence of God inside every person, and on individual, silent communion with the spirit of God. Quakers believed strongly, sometimes fanatically, in equality and human rights, and they protested slavery, war, and poverty, devoting most of their time to social welfare and education. When they arrived in New England, they became the Native Americans' best friends. It is easy to understand — given the stern, rigid beliefs of the white, mainstream Protestant society of the day — why the Quakers were widely regarded as misguided troublemakers.

New England's strict and moral Puritans (their name came from their efforts to cleanse the English Protestant church of Catholic and governmental interference) hated the Quakers for holding beliefs different from Puritan teaching. The Puritans began punishing and imprisoning Quakers whenever they could. They were flogged with knotted whips, locked up in filthy cells without water or food, had their ears cut off — all done by church-going Christians simply because the Quakers were preaching a humanitarian message of their own. During the American Revolution, patriots regularly attacked Quakers because they opposed the war on the grounds that violence was never justified.

Mary Dyer was an outspoken Quaker from Rhode Island who incurred the wrath of the authorities in Massachusetts. She had been warned about entering the colony, and on one of her visits she was seized. She was tied up and taken to a gallows and forced to watch the hanging of two friends. Then she was blindfolded and prepared for execution. But the authorities decided against executing her and sent her back to Rhode Island. Determined to have her say, Dyer returned to Boston. On Boston Common, she was brought to the gallows again. She would be saved, her captors told her, if she left Massachusetts for good. "Nay, I cannot," she said. "In obedience to the will of the Lord God I came and in his will I abide faithful to death." This time, she was hanged.[4]

Despite the persecutions, Quakers persevered. William Penn, a distinguished leader of the sect, founded Pennsylvania as a haven of religious and political freedom. Philadelphia, nicknamed Quaker City, was the place where the Declaration of Independence was signed and the U.S. Constitution was adopted. It was also the capital of the new United States from 1790 to 1800. Today, the American Friends Service Committee continues to support humanitarian causes. Although the Friends are among the world's smallest denominations, they are enormously respected for the good works they do and are a fine example of how a group that has known the pain of discrimination and prejudice can rise above it all.

The story of the Mormons (The Church of Jesus Christ of Latter-day Saints) is another such example. They, too, marched to a different drummer and were punished for it by their fellow Christians. And, like the Friends, the Mormons managed to overcome the hostility to become influential and respected members of society.

The Mormon Church was founded in 1830 from unlikely beginnings for a religion with worldwide influence. As the story goes, fourteen-year-old Joseph Smith, who lived on a farm in Palmyra, New York, had visions of an angel named Moroni. Moroni sent him to a nearby hillside to find a set of golden plates inscribed with Egyptian hieroglyphics, which were buried there. Smith found the plates and translated them with the help of two special stones that Moroni also provided. Smith's translation eventually took form as the Book of Mormon, the Mormon's "Golden Bible."

The Book of Mormon told of a lost tribe of Israelites who came to America hundreds of years before Christ was born and were the ancestors of the Native Americans. After Jesus's death, the Book said, he visited America to establish his church. But the first church members were destroyed in a war — all but Moroni, who hid the golden plates. The Book of Mormon also prophesied that the Mormon Church would rise again in America and that its "latter-day saints" would see to it that the misinformation taught by other churches would be corrected.

Again, it is easy to see why the vast majority of Christians, whose faith was rooted in the Bible's traditional and ancient teachings, should be disturbed by an "upstart" religion they believed was the figment of a teenager's vivid imagination. To escape the wrath of his neighbors, Smith moved his new church to Ohio, where he was tarred and feathered by an angry mob and his colleagues severely beaten. Smith then went to Missouri, but it was no better there. The state militia and a band of vigilantes attacked his community, leaving seventeen Mormons dead. Smith escaped to Illinois, and it was there, in 1844, while he was in jail, that a lynch mob broke into his cell, dragged him outside, and hanged him.

Smith was now a martyr as well as a prophet. He was succeeded by Brigham Young, one of America's great frontiersmen. Young took his Mormons on a difficult trek to Utah, which was not then a state, and settled Salt Lake City, where Mormon world headquarters is today. Young became governor of the territory, but he literally had to fight to keep Utah and his church together, and its members alive. The practice of polygamy — having more than one wife or husband — by a few Mormons further antagonized non-Mormon settlers, and soon the U.S. government sent troops to Utah to get rid of Young. The Mormon War that followed lasted about a year, and when it was over, the Mormon Church was stronger than ever. Mormons appeased many of their critics by abolishing polygamy, and when Utah became a state in 1896, they were in firm control, a situation that holds to this day.

Looking at the Friends and the Mormons, one has to ask whether their unorthodox views justified all the hatred and the terrible violence directed against them. What, really, had members of these sects ever done to warrant such a response? When someone refuses to renounce his or her faith, should that person be executed, as Mary Dyer was on Boston Common? Because Joseph Smith's ideas ran counter to those of other Christians, did that call for a hanging? Is being against war and in favor of human rights a crime? Does polygamy justify sending in armed soldiers? Can we truly say that a fourteen-year-old boy's vision of an angel was a hoax? After all, many Christians believe that various saints had visions; many believe in mystical experiences and in the seemingly impossible miracles Christ performed. And what about the story of Saint Paul, converted on his way to Damascus when a brilliant light shot down from heaven and blinded him? Many Christians believe the voice he heard was that of Jesus. Mohammed, too, reportedly saw an angel who told him to read from a sacred scroll. Can we truly say, as some people do, that Mohammed was a fraud? Why do we accept some things and not others? Are differences of opinion, claims to possess the truth, or different approaches to performing good works reasons to persecute someone?

For a non-Mormon who finds it difficult to accept Moroni and the Book of Mormon, and for a non-Quaker who needs a formal creed to live by, a good deal of effort to be understanding is required. We must look closely at the missions of all the faiths we hear about. We have to be willing to accept the evidence, when it appears, that faiths other than our own are well intentioned. We must learn a bit more about other religions, perhaps drawing up a list of the stereotypes we've associated with each and then looking more closely at them. We must learn to be comfortable with and to live with other religions. Forget the ridiculous old expression "Never discuss religion and politics." Why shouldn't we? Discussion is how we communicate and understand. Without it we simmer in silence, sopping up wrong-headed ideas, and out of that comes prejudice.

It cannot be true that there is only one road to salvation. If that were the case, a cruel joke will have been played on everyone who lives a decent life but is not on that road. It is also not true that all Catholics, all Protestants, all Jews, or all Muslims think and act in the same way. If that were so, we would not have the deep divisions and the various branches that exist in almost every major and minor faith known to humankind. Years ago, Catholics were not allowed to enter a Protestant church or a synagogue or read the King James version of the Bible. They were not permitted to do those things because many Catholics didn't understand what Protestants and Jews were all about, or maybe they were afraid they'd be enticed away from their own faith. Today, many Catholics are very comfortable learning about other faiths, even participating in other services, and for many years the Vatican and the Protestant World Council of Churches have been holding discussions in an effort to repair the damage done by centuries of misunderstanding. Not so long ago, a rabbi would never have been invited to preach a sermon in any Christian church. Today, rabbis and other Jewish leaders meet with the pope and Vatican officials. Protestants once found it hard to believe that a Catholic holding public office could ever make a decision on birth control or abortion without being influenced by the church, which opposes both. Today, Catholic governors and senators are willing to risk angering their church by favoring birth control and a woman's right to choose an abortion. And for a long time, any discussion of Islam in a Christian church would be confined to sermons about battles between Crusaders and the Knights of the Crescent. Today, in many church-sponsored symposia on Islam, a parishioner is made to feel more like a student in a comparative religion class than a warrior for his or her faith.

One man who saw the necessity of dialogue between the faiths was Pope John XXIII. A simple man of remarkable vision and understanding, John was responsible for an enormously important meeting called the Second Vatican Council. From 1962 until 1965, the Council not only modernized the Catholic church's religious rites but condemned anti-Semitism and called for more dialogue between the church and Protestant and Eastern Orthodox churches. The last goal was embodied in what we call ecumenism, or the spirit of cooperation and unity. Pope John was, thus, a visionary and a reformer, just as Martin Luther was.

It's doubtful than any one of us will have the impact of a Luther or a John in our daily activities, nor will we, individually, wipe out religious intolerance and prejudice on a global scale. But we can certainly speak up when someone ridicules another's faith. We can also learn not to sneer at other belief systems, and we can learn to defend our own without running down someone else's. We can try to understand that it's far better to understand another's beliefs than to try to convert him or her to ours.

Imagine a choir with members of many faiths. Its strength is in its unity, its spirit of cooperation, its blending of all kinds of voices, and the universal message about God and love, joy and peace, that it sends out in song. Religious prejudice, and all other forms of bigotry, would be impossible if more of the world's people behaved as a choir.

4 • JEWS
Eternal Outsiders

Let my people go!
— Moses, Exodus 5:1

None but members of the Nation may be citizens of the state. None but those of German blood, whatever their creed, may be members of the Nation. No Jew, therefore, may be a member of the Nation.
— From the Nazi Party's 25-point program of 1920

If you are Jewish, you are painfully aware of the slurs and the outright discrimination that have been directed against your ancestors and perhaps even against you and your family. If you are not Jewish, you may not have paid much attention to what Jews have had to endure for centuries, or, worse, you may even have made remarks yourself or used nicknames that are anti-Semitic. (The term *anti-Semitic* is widely used to mean anti-Jew. Actually, *Semitic* refers to Semites, a group of people that includes Arabs and, in ancient times, the Babylonians, Assyrians, and Phoenicians.)

Although, as we have seen, many religious groups have suffered because of the venomous tongues and the cruel, irrational actions of bigots, few have been subjected to such widespread — and indeed it is a global phenomenon — and such long-standing abuse as Jews and the ancient Hebrews, the collection of wandering Semitic tribes mentioned in the Bible and from whom the Jews sprang and to whom they are culturally united by religion.

(The name Jew is suggested by the Hebrew word *Yehudhi,* which means a member of the Hebrew tribe of Judah, and also by the Latin word *Judaeus,* which means a person who lived in Judea, the ancient name for southern Palestine.)

For centuries, the Jews, to put it mildly, have not had easy lives. Ever since Roman legions wiped out the Jewish nation and razed its glorious capital, Jerusalem, in the year 70 A.D., the Jews have been forced to wander throughout the non-Jewish world, often treated as foreigners even in countries where they were born. Jews were persecuted by ancient Egyptian kings and forced into slavery a thousand and more years before the birth of Jesus. Babylonian Jews were barred from holding political office, bearing arms, and building synagogues and were forced to wear yellow identification patches. Every European country during the Middle Ages either drove out Jews or confined them to city ghettos. In Spain, they were forced to convert to Christianity to save their lives and were prohibited from holding positions in which they could impose penalties on Christians. Jews were falsely accused of causing the devastating plague known as the Black Death by poisoning Christian wells; they were barred in many countries from holding property or citizenship and from hiring Christians as servants. During the Nazi years of World War II, they again suffered enormously in what stands as one of the most heinous crimes against humanity: millions were gassed to death in concentration camps. The hatred has still not disappeared. Even today, Jews are reviled by their neighbors in the troubled Middle East, by new Nazis in Germany, or, in America, simply by people who live next door or who share the same office. As a tongue-in-cheek headline in the New York City newspaper, *The Village Voice,* put it, "God Must Have Loved Anti-Semites, He Made So Many of Them."

Why has such hostility been directed toward this one people? What could they possibly have done to deserve such horrid treatment? Why today does even the word *Jew* so often take on a contemptible quality?

Before we try to answer those questions, a bit of background about the Jews and their religion, Judaism, might be helpful. According to the Bible, Abraham was the father and founder of the people we know as Hebrews. Around 2000 B.C., Abraham emigrated to the land of Canaan, an area in the Middle East that became Palestine. Abraham worshiped one God, Jehovah, something that no one else had done. The belief in one God spread and was solidified a few hundred years later when, according to the Bible, Moses, the lawgiver and judge of the Hebrews, was given the Ten Commandments by God on Mount Sinai. The first of those commandments was "Thou shalt have no other gods before me."

This strong belief in one all-powerful, indestructible, and personal God was what set the Jews apart from all other religions — and what eventually made Judaism and the Ten Commandments the root of Christianity. Religious Jews believe in an afterlife, in God's hand in all things, that humans are created in God's image, and in doing good deeds. Jews are taught to love and imitate God and to love their fellow human beings — all teachings familiar to many of those who practice other faiths.

Religious differences were perhaps one reason for the early persecution of the Hebrews who settled in Egypt, especially those under the rule of Ramses II. They were treated as serfs — "in bondage," as they were to refer to the experience later — and forced to make bricks and do other forms of manual labor; at one time, all male Hebrew children were ordered killed. The Hebrews' distinct religious beliefs and "alien" tribal ways may have disturbed the pharaohs. The unknown, whether it be a mysterious pain or a stranger, is often feared. People also become suspicious of foreign practices or people they do not know, and they quite often assume the worst without any proof or on the slightest evidence. So it might have been with the Egyptians, who had their own gods and their own stern beliefs. They may have regarded the Hebrew religion with its one God who was both a creator and a lawgiver to be worshiped alone an insult or threat to a pharaoh who had such an impressive title as Son of the Sun.

The Romans, too, suffered from arrogance that comes with power. Roman governors in Palestine were disrespectful of the Jewish religion, and when the Jews rebelled against their authority, the Romans responded with crushing force.

But the pharaohs and the Roman generals and governors are

part of ancient history in a special part of the world. The Middle East, the original home of the Jewish people, has for centuries been torn by civil wars, revolts, and invasions, by religious, cultural, and political differences, by jealousies, clannishness, and the desire for power. It is not surprising that the Jews, who have long been a part of that turbulent scene, would suffer along with all of the other people in the eastern Mediterranean area and that they would make many enemies.

One has to wonder, though, why the Jews have been singled out so often for persecution outside of the turbulent Middle East and by people they have never threatened or warred against. Why has the hatred persisted for so many centuries? There are any number of theories to explain the phenomenon we know as anti-Semitism — everything from the discredited notion that Jews are actually inferior in physical makeup and character and should be prevented from mingling their blood with purer stocks of people, to economic rivalry and envy and resentment of Jewish success in business, to the Jews' refusal to believe that Jesus was the Messiah, to the tendency of people during periods of insecurity to find a convenient scapegoat in a member of an alien, isolated, perhaps defenseless, minority. Some people in Europe did not like Jews because many of them opposed the monarchies or the Catholic church's influence on the state; Jews were disliked because some of them were tax collectors or moneylenders who charged high interest; in the U.S., many people associated Jews with membership in the Communist Party or radical political groups. Nowadays, many blacks tend to distrust Jews, especially when they are landlords or operate businesses in black neighborhoods. Many non-Jews, it seems, can always find a reason to dislike Jews, can always find something to blame them for.

It is not possible in these few pages to examine all of the reasons in depth, no more than it is possible to detail here the rich history of the Jews. We can, however, outline briefly the history of anti-Semitism, and perhaps, by recounting several noteworthy incidents, shed some light on this atrocious form of prejudice and demonstrate just how irrational it is. As you read ahead, you will see that in virtually every instance of prejudice, simply being Jewish is no justification whatsoever for persecution. It should also be clear that the more one repeats all the myths and misconceptions about the Jews, the more they become acceptable and believable.

It is an understatement to say that negative images of the Jews are common. Certainly, William Shakespeare's play *The Merchant of Venice* contributed to the stereotype of Jews as hard-hearted, money-grubbing people. The central character in the play is Shylock, a greedy Jewish moneylender. Shakespeare describes him as "A stony adversary, an inhuman wretch/Uncapable of pity, void and empty/From any dreams of mercy." Shylock loans the merchant Antonio some money for a few months on the condition that if it is not paid back in time, Shylock will be allowed to cut a pound of flesh from Antonio's body. Antonio is unable to pay off the loan, and Shylock claims his pound of flesh at a trial. He is told he may take it — but in so doing is not allowed to shed a single drop of blood, nor must he cut off more or less than an exact pound. If he does not follow those impossible directions, then he will lose his life. Shylock, naturally, gives up his outrageous claim but is fined heavily for trying to take the life of a Venetian citizen.

An even harsher portrayal of Jews came from Martin Luther, the renowned German leader of the Protestant Reformation. A forceful speaker and writer, Luther left no doubt about how he felt Jews should be treated. "First," he said, "their synagogues should be set on fire, and whatever does not burn up should be covered or spread over with dirt so that no one may ever be able to see a cinder or stone of it." Then, he went on, Jews should be "put under one roof, or in a stable, like Gypsies, in order that they may realize that they are not masters in our land." Luther called Jews "poisonous bitter worms" who should be stripped of all their belongings "which they have extorted usuriously from us," and driven out of the country forever.[1] There is bitter irony in such statements, considering that Jesus was a Jew and that Judaism is the mother of Christianity.

Perhaps one clue to such a bitter denunciation of the Jews may be found in the legend of the Wandering Jew and in a number of versions of it. In the stories, which originated in medieval Europe, the Wandering Jew is sometimes depicted as a cobbler in the time of Jesus, sometimes as the doorkeeper in Pontius Pilate's court.

According to the legend, when Jesus, struggling under the weight of his cross on his way to Calvary, passed the Jew's home, the Jew refused to allow him to rest and cruelly told him to move faster. Jesus is supposed to have replied, "Truly I go away, and that quickly, but thou shalt tarry til I come." Thus, the Jew was condemned to roam the earth until Judgment Day — the legend says that he does not die but keeps coming back at about the age of thirty, wiser and more repentant each time.

The tale was extremely popular in Europe in medieval times, and many people claimed to have actually seen the Wandering Jew, who became a symbol of the Jewish people, doomed to wander the world because they rejected the notion of Jesus as Messiah. The Jews believed in the coming of a Messiah, the promised savior of humankind, but they did not accept Jesus as the deliverer.

According to the Bible's New Testament, when Jesus presented himself as the Son of God before the Jewish authorities, they regarded his words as blasphemy, a crime demanding the death penalty. They handed him over to the Roman authorities, the only ones who could impose such a sentence. The charge of blasphemy in itself might not be enough to have Jesus put to death by the pagan Romans, so the Jewish leaders reportedly emphasized his claim to be King of the Jews, a claim that meant treason against Rome. According to the Bible, Pontius Pilate, a Roman official and governor of the Jews, was not convinced that Jesus was guilty as charged. He asked Jesus if he were indeed King of the Jews, and Jesus replied, "Thou sayest it."

The Bible says that Pilate tried several times to save Jesus but finally, perhaps to appease the people who were pressuring him to execute the self-proclaimed Messiah who would deliver mankind from its sins, Pilate ordered his execution on the cross. But before he did so, Pilate washed his hands in public in a symbolic gesture that meant he bore no responsibility for Jesus's fate.

Familiar as it may be to many of us, the Gospels' version of this story is clouded by the centuries and by the scarcity of historical sources. Jesus himself wrote nothing, and no original writings by his disciples exist. We know nothing of his life between the age of twelve to the time he was around thirty. The four Gospels,

Matthew, Mark, Luke, and John, and the epistles of the New Testament, are the primary sources for his life, and these were written after Jesus's death by followers who were trying to convert people to their beliefs. Only a few references to Jesus are made in Jewish writings from the time, and none of the Roman historians of the time mention Jesus by name, although a few used the word *Christos* when describing Roman persecution of his religious movement.

The scantiness of the information about Jesus has resulted in various descriptions of his life and his relationship to the Jewish people and in numerous interpretations of his teachings. Interpretations can be made to suit the aims of a group, sometimes at the expense of another. For instance, the early Christian church sternly blamed the Jews for Jesus's death and tended to portray Pilate as a sensitive judge who tried desperately to save him. Christians interpreted Pilate's washing of his hands as an indication that he was shifting responsibility for Jesus's death to the Jews. When he gave in to the Jewish mob, according to the gospel of Matthew, the Jews accepted the responsibility with the words, "His blood be on us and on our children."

Historians debate Pilate's role in the crucifixion, and several have suggested that it seems highly unlikely that the governor, whose record of cruelty and ruthlessness was well known, could have regarded Jesus, a Jewish rebel, with any kindness whatsoever. Whatever his reasons — and certainly Jesus's claim to kingship must have irritated Pilate no end — it was he who signed Jesus's death warrant. He may have done so at the urging of some Jewish leaders, but certainly not because of any nationwide call among Jews for his death. After all, Jesus was born a Jew and died one. As Abram Sachar, the late president of Brandeis University wrote:

> At no time during his ministry, even in his most iconoclastic moments, had he any intention of separating himself from his people. Throughout his ministry he toiled to enrich their spirit by bringing to them, and to them alone, the inner meaning of the prophetic messages. The Gentile world was out of his ken. "I was not sent," he said when

> asked to heal the daughter of a Canaanite woman, "except to the lost sheep of the house of Israel." His disciples were Jews too, loyal to Jewish traditions and abiding by the commandments.[2]

Still, the Jews' unfortunate reputation as Christ killers, the people of "deicide," is hard to dispel among some Christians even today. Even the name of a plant, butcher's bloom, is evidence of the lingering stereotype: it is also known as Jew's myrtle because it supposedly formed the crown of thorns placed by the Jews on Jesus's head. Blaming a whole group for the death of Jesus seems, of course, absurd nowadays, just as ridiculous as blaming all Germans for the Holocaust or all Muslims for the massacres that some carried out against Christians. But in Europe in the Middle Ages especially, the notion that Jews were a damned people because they bore responsibility for Jesus's death was very strong. In fact, persecution of the Jews in Christian countries at that time was not only condoned but considered Christian duty. Given the fact that Christianity is a religion that preaches love and compassion, the behavior of non-Jews during the Middle Ages made a hollow mockery of the faith that Jesus's followers founded. Monarchs enriched themselves by confiscating Jewish property and sent the Jews away. King Edward I of England and Charles VI of France were among those who expelled their Jewish subjects or turned them into beggars. In France, lawmakers made a rule that "Jews and harlots" could not touch bread or fruit in shops and markets. In some European countries, Christians were executed for marrying Jews. During Passover, when Jews used to mark their doorways with lamb's blood to repel the Angel of Death, Jews were accused of using the blood of murdered Christian children. Pope Innocent III (a rather unfortunate name considering his view that all Jews were doomed to slavery forever because they crucified Christ) ordered all Jews to wear distinctive badges of yellow cloth.[3] It is no wonder that in Spain many fearful Jews embraced Christianity, or professed to do so, to avoid execution. Jews who converted were called Conversos, and many said they were Christian but secretly remained faithful to Judaic principles. The Spanish Inquisition — the Roman Catholic church's tribunal that hunted down and punished people who held opinions contrary to church teaching — persecuted the Conversos. Soldiers of the Inquisition, with the support of high government officials and several popes, arrested suspects in the dead of night, chained them in dungeons, tortured them, and after secret trials, burned many of them at the stake. In a most hypocritical argument, the church maintained that burning heretics — those who disagreed with church teaching — did not violate the church's axiom to remain "untainted with blood" because, technically, burning did not shed any blood.

In all fairness, it must be pointed out that not all religious and secular rulers hated the Jews. Periods of persecution were often followed by long periods of tolerance and cooperation. In Italy, for example, despite the attitude of a few Vatican councils, the church generally protected Jews as the keepers of the Old Testament's laws. Pope Gregory I barred the practice of forcing Jews to convert to Christianity, and he upheld their right to citizenship. "Do not allow the Jews to be molested in the performance of their services," he wrote to a bishop of Naples. "Let them have full liberty to observe and keep all their festivals and holy days, as both they and their fathers have done for so long."[4] Pope Innocent IV, more tolerant than his predecessor, threw out the legend of the ritual murder of Christian children by Jews. Before the horrors of the Spanish Inquisition, from about the ninth to the twelfth century, the Jews enjoyed a truly golden era in Spain, then a Muslim country, and made notable contributions to literature, poetry, philosophy, and finance. Among the shining lights of the era was Moses Maimonides, the influential philosopher, physician, and jurist, the "light of the West," of whom it was said, "From Moses the lawgiver unto Moses Maimonides, there has been none like unto Moses." Although the favored position of the Jews in Spain was to end when the Muslim rulers were driven from the country by Catholic monarchs, the richness and the variety of their culture left indelible marks.

By the time Oliver Cromwell came to power as lord protector of England in the mid-1600s, Jews, at least in some parts of the Western world, were treated well once again. Cromwell encouraged Jewish migration to England, and the French National Assembly also opened their country to Jews. In Colonial America, too, Jews were encouraged to settle by men like Roger Williams, the clergyman who founded Rhode Island, which became the most tolerant community in the world at the time. During the American Revolution, there were around 2,000 Jews in the New England colonies, and most of them distinguished themselves as merchants and financiers. Haym Salomon, for one, was a wealthy Polish exile who was jailed as a spy by the British when the Revolution began. He escaped, established a banking business in Philadelphia, and became one of the leading financers of George Washington's army. He even helped a number of struggling politicians, among them James Madison, who was to become the fourth president of the United States. Wrote Madison: "The kindness of our little friend . . . is a fund which will preserve me from extremities, but I never resort to it without great mortification, as he obstinately rejects all recompense."[5]

But all too soon, the Jews would once again fall out of favor. Life was especially difficult for those in eastern Europe, primarily in Poland and Russia, in the late 1700s and 1800s. Jews were forced to live in certain areas, and severe restrictions were placed on what they could study and what kind of work they could do. Every so often, the government would organize massacres of Jews, called pogroms. (The word *pogrom* is Russian for devastation.) Hundreds of thousands of Jews died in the pogroms or had their property looted or destroyed. Supposedly, the massacres were the response of irate Christians who wanted to punish the Jews for their anti-Christ attitudes and for their alleged ritual killing of Christian babies. In reality, however, the pogroms were orchestrated by the czarist government, which wanted to divert the attention of Russian workers and peasants who were discontented with the harsh political and economic conditions of the regime. The workers were all too ready to blame the Jews for their unhappiness, and by getting the workers to take out their anger on the Jews, the repressive regime thought it could defuse any attempts to topple the government. And once again, there was confirmation that whenever there is underlying racial hatred and religious bias, someone is always ready and able to tap into such poison and use it to advantage.

The murderous pogroms continued even after the Russian Revolution eventually did overthrow the czarist government. Although the persecution subsided after the revolution, so-called

White Guards in the Ukraine massacred hundreds of thousands of Jews. The relative calm that followed was to last only a few years, however, because the seeds of the greatest pogrom of all, the Nazi government's "final solution of the Jewish problem," were already being sown.

While the pogroms were underway in the late 1800s, another anti-Semitic event was playing itself out in France. It was known as the Dreyfus affair, and it became a monumental scandal that would eventually discredit the French military, monarchy, and the church. Captain Alfred Dreyfus was a French artillery officer and a Jew who was convicted in 1894 of betraying military secrets to Germany. The damning "evidence" was a list of sensitive documents, addressed to the German military attaché in Paris, in handwriting that was similar to Dreyfus's. Dreyfus protested his innocence, but his bigoted judges disagreed and convicted him of high treason. He was sentenced to life imprisonment on Devil's Island, the notorious French penal colony off Guiana.

There is little doubt that French anti-Semitism put Dreyfus in prison. The French military was a hotbed of anti-Jewish feelings, and Jewish officers were often insulted and drawn into duels with other officers. While Dreyfus was on trial and all through his imprisonment, French society was fiercely divided over his case. The military, supporters of the government, and many Catholics believed Dreyfus was guilty; socialists, those who favored a republican government, and people who opposed church involvement in governmental affairs, felt Dreyfus was innocent. Among those in the officer's camp was the novelist Emile Zola, who published an open letter in a newspaper. The letter, under the heading "J'accuse" ("I accuse"), charged that the military and the government were covering up the truth in the affair.

Eventually, evidence surfaced that the damning list of secrets had been written by someone else, and Dreyfus was cleared. It was not until 1906, however, that he was reinstated in the army with a promotion. A year later, Dreyfus resigned. But the affair was still not over. In 1908, Dreyfus was shot and wounded by an anti-Semitic journalist.

The Dreyfus affair was not only a blot on the French military and the French government, but it also sorely weakened the Catholic church's influence in the country. Because of its anti-Semitic views, the church lost its status as the state church of France through the so-called Law of Separation. The Dreyfus affair also stimulated the movement known as Zionism, the belief that Jews should have their own nation. The man who founded the movement, Theodor Herzl, was a newspaper reporter who covered the Dreyfus trial. Before the trial, Herzl believed that the best way to deal with anti-Semitism was for the Jews to become part of Christian Europe. But the trial convinced him that the only answer was for the Jews to become a separate people, with their own land. Herzl was, of course, among those who had the greatest influence in the movement that resulted in the creation of the State of Israel in 1948.

The Dreyfus affair was a notorious miscarriage of justice, and the officer's imprisonment on Devil's Island was a degradation, but he was able to emerge from it, perhaps a stronger man. Such has often been the case down through the ages with the Jewish people. During their periods of persecution in Europe, when they were forbidden to work at professions or were barred from owning large businesses, Jews had to earn a living as best they could. Most were forced to become peddlers, traders, or tailors. They managed to make money, and they made more money by lending it to others, and eventually they dominated banking and finance in many countries. They also knew the value of education, which, along with money, was to become their way out of misery. As the historian Will Durant wrote:

> In every age the soul of the Jew has been torn between the resolve to make his way in a hostile world, and his hunger for the goods of the mind. A Jewish merchant is a dead scholar; he envies and generously honors the man who, escaping the fever of wealth, pursues in peace the love of learning and the mirage of wisdom.[6]

Education and money may have been a way up the ladder, but they have never quite managed to dispel the hostility. Even as Jews became successful and influential in the financial offices of government and banks, they became a natural target for those who disliked taxes and bankers — and Jews. Again, Will Durant:

> The days of peace were made anxious by the ever-present danger of pogroms; and every Jew had to learn by heart the prayer to be recited in the moment of martyrdom. The pursuit of wealth was made more feverish by the harassed insecurity of its gains; the gibes of [street urchins] were ever ready to greet the wearers of the yellow badge. . . . For that one death on the cross how many crucifixions?[7]

How many indeed? Everywhere the Jews went, it was the same story: waves of anti-Semitism, organized or subtle, followed by periods of tolerance, some of it grudging, followed by another wave of antagonism, perhaps touched off by some incident in which a Jew "overstepped his bounds." Moreover, the anti-Jewish sentiment was not confined to Europe. America, too, played a part in the familiar scenario, although with the notable exception of the Ku Klux Klan, anti-Semitism here was not organized but most often took the form of social discrimination.

Waves of Jews had flocked to the United States after the pogroms: between 1880 and 1920, more than 2.5 million Jews came here from areas under Russian domination. They were never forced to live in ghettos nor had to fear pogroms, nor was there much if any of the "Christ killer" hatred of Europe, but they did face resentment (the same kind that was directed against all aliens here) and often banded together in neighborhoods that became predominantly, and comfortably, Jewish. Jews were barred from membership in country clubs, from certain resort areas, from high-level positions in many corporations, even from debutante cotillions. Immigration acts in the early 1920s put strict limits on the number of people who could come to the U.S. from eastern Europe, an area with a large Jewish population. According to the bigots, all Jews were rich and powerful, or Communists, or trouble-making liberals.

One well-known American who contributed to the Jews' troubles here was the automaker Henry Ford. In his newspaper, the *Dearborn Independent,* he reprinted an offensive and inflammatory tract called "The Protocols of the Elder of Zion." The published material, written in Russia during one of the pogroms, supposedly revealed secret Jewish plans to dominate the world by eroding the morals and health of non-Jews and by raking over all international financial affairs. Eventually, the protocols were shown to be forgeries and were wholly discredited. Henry Ford later apologized for his anti-Semitism and for printing the lies.

The protocols may have been laid to rest in America, but not so in Germany. While American Jews were being insulted by a more covert form of discrimination, things were turning ugly under the National Socialist (shortened to Nazi) Party of Adolf Hitler. One of the world's most vicious dictators and probably the world's arch-anti-Semite, Hitler became chancellor of Germany in 1933 and led the country until his death at the end of World War II. Hitler used the protocols as one of his justifications for persecuting the Jews, even though he knew it was a myth.

The tragic story of the Nazi persecution of the Jews has been told many times, and it bears repeating. For years, European Jews had held influential positions in business and made enormous contributions to culture, science, and politics. But whenever there was economic distress or political upheaval, they were made the scapegoats. During the 1930s and 1940s, when Hitler's propaganda machine regularly cranked out all manner of vicious racist doctrine, Jews were vilified as wealthy capitalists, cowardly traitors, and misers. Their property was confiscated, and they were denied the protection of German law. Young Jewish women were called promiscuous and were accused of spreading sexually transmitted diseases. Newspaper cartoons caricatured physical features associated with being Jewish, notably the hooked nose. Jewish children could not play with non-Jewish children, Jewish mothers could not shop in Christian-owned stores. And through it all, Hitler's chilling slogan was repeated over and over by the racist press and by many German citizens: "Anti-Semites of the world, unite! People of Europe, free yourselves!"

Bad as all that was, it paled in comparison to what would follow. In Warsaw, Poland, Nazi governors set up a ghetto, a walled-off part of the city, into which more than 400,000 Jews were herded. Disease and starvation awaited them there, and more than 300 died every day. One of the Nazi governors gloated, "The Jews will perish by hunger and misery, and of the Jewish question only a cemetery will remain." By 1943, only about 65,000 Jews remained in the ghetto. The survivors decided to revolt. With smuggled weapons, they fought back, but were no match for the more than 1,000 Nazi soldiers who attacked with planes, tanks, and flamethrowers. Some 20,000 men, women, and children were burned to death. The survivors were sent to the infamous death camps the Nazis had organized.

Jews who were sent to the camps performed slave labor, but many of them were killed there. Death was actually the goal. It was to be a genocide, the deliberate destruction of a group of people, in this case the Jews. The names of the camps where the systematic massacres took place are known throughout the world, among them Dachau, Buchenwald, and Bergen-Belsen in Germany, and Treblinka and Auschwitz in Poland.

At the end of World War II, American and allied soldiers took over the camps and freed any prisoners who were left alive. But the joy the liberated prisoners expressed could never make up for the shocking sights the soldiers witnessed. Heaps and heaps of rotting corpses of Jewish men, women, and children were everywhere. There were gas chambers, which the prison guards had forced Jews to enter — on the pretext the prisoners were to take showers. Instead of a spray of water, a mist of poison gas was released into the chambers, killing the prisoners. There were furnaces, built by bakers, in which the naked bodies of the dead Jewish prisoners were burned. The Allied soldiers found cartons full of gold fillings taken from the teeth of the victims, lamp shades made of human skin, soap made from human fat. And there were the horror stories the emaciated survivors told: of prisoners drowned so doctors could study the effects of water on human lungs, of sterilizations, of starvation and torture, of prisoners forced to dig their own graves before being machine-gunned to death or ripped to pieces by dogs.

The words of one survivor give us an idea of what went on in a Nazi concentration camp:

> The girls with long hair went to be shaved; those who had short hair went with the men, straight into the gas chambers. . . . I was standing in the yard, together with a group left behind for digging graves, and was looking at

> my sisters, my brothers and friends being pushed to their deaths. . . .
>
> Ukrainian SS men counted 750 people to each chamber [the SS was a unit of Nazis who originally served as body guards to Hitler and who later became security guards in charge of exterminating undesirables], and those who did not want to enter were stabbed with bayonets and forced inside. There was blood everywhere. I heard the doors being locked, the moaning, shouting and cries of despair in Polish and Jewish; the crying of the children and women which made the blood run cold in my veins. . . .
>
> We pulled out the corpses of those who were alive only a short time ago, we pulled them using leather belts to the huge mass graves while the camp orchestra played, played from morning till night.[8]

By the time the war was over and the Nazis defeated, Hitler and several of his henchmen had committed suicide. But they had succeeded in wiping out nearly six million Jews — two-thirds to three-quarters of all the Jews in Europe, half of the world's entire Jewish population. Never in all history had there been anything like the Holocaust. Among the many who died in the camps in those terrible years was a young woman named Anne Frank, whose diary, begun while she was forced to hide from the Nazis in a back apartment in Amsterdam in 1942, is a classic account of how it was to live under the Nazi occupation. "I feel wicked sleeping in a warm bed," Frank wrote,

> while my dearest friends have been knocked down or have fallen into a gutter somewhere out in the cold night. I get frightened when I think of close friends who have now been delivered into the hands of the cruelest brutes that walk the earth. And all because they are Jews!"[9]

In November of 1945, the United States and its allies convened an international military tribunal. Each of the victorious countries — the U.S., Great Britain, France, and the Soviet Union — provided judges for the tribunal, which put many of the top Nazis on trial in Nuremberg, Germany. Charged with crimes against humanity, ten of the Nazis were hanged, and several others were sentenced to life in prison. One of those brought to trial was Hermann Goering, commandant of the German Air Force. Goering was to be hanged, but he committed suicide by taking poison he had hidden in his prison cell.

There are those who feel the story of the Holocaust should be allowed to just die away, that there is no need to continually recount the horrors of the Nazi regime because they happened a long time ago and focusing on them serves little purpose other than to stir up hatred for Germans who were not even born when Hitler was in power.

But we cannot simply let bygones be bygones when it comes to the colossal pogrom that Hitler organized. That it was a horrid crime against humanity goes without saying. We cannot forget it, nor should we. The Greek statesman Demosthenes tells us, "Even if the time for action has gone by, the time for extracting a lesson from history is ever at hand for those who are wise." By never forgetting what the Nazis did to the Jews, we may be less apt to repeat their awful crimes.

We say *may be* because even so awful an event as the Holocaust has failed to put an end to anti-Semitism. Some people — perhaps they are not the ones "who are wise," as Demosthenes put it — still believe that the massacres in the death camps were exaggerated, and some even go so far as to say none of it ever happened at all. In 1991, during a memorial in Romania, where years ago police and soldiers conducted a pogrom that killed 8,000 Jews, a middle-aged, well-dressed woman disrupted the ceremonies by shouting, "Lies! The Jews didn't die. We won't allow Romanians to be insulted by foreigners in their own country."[10] Even more shocking was the recent report of a home video game making the rounds in Austria and Germany. Called KZ Manager (KZ is short for the German word for concentration camp), the game features a graphic of a castlelike building with a swastika (the Nazi Party's symbol) and a chimney belching smoke on top. In the game, the player is the commandant of the Treblinka death camp and earns points by gassing prisoners and by selling gold fillings and human-skin lamp shades. While the game often substitutes Turks for Jews (many Turks work in Germany), it is undoubtedly based on the Nazi genocide and contains anti-Semitic remarks. Other games, among them one called Aryan Test, refer to the Jews directly. Aryan Test claims it is manufactured by Adolf Hitler Software Ltd. and another, Anti-Turk Test, says it is manufactured in Buchenwald by Hitler and Hess. (Rudolf Hess, a trusted aide to Hitler, was sentenced to life imprisonment at the Nuremberg trials.)[11]

There are numerous other examples of current anti-Semitism, and hardly a day goes by when an incident is not reported in the press. We read and hear of vandals smashing hundreds of tombstones in a Jewish cemetery in Argentina, a country with Latin America's largest Jewish population; of swastikas painted on a Jewish family's front door somewhere near where you live; of kids in Germany with shaved heads shouting, "Heil, Hitler"; of Jews being denied the right to leave the Soviet Union; of a synagogue's Torah, a scroll on which is written Jewish law and wisdom, desecrated; of Columbia University in New York City referred to as Columbia Jewniversity.

Ironically, some of the anti-Jewish expression comes from people who, one would think, should know better. We hear of anti-Semitism among blacks, a people who have been on the receiving end of so much hatred. There is, for example, Louis Farrakhan, a Black Muslim leader whose speeches have often been branded as anti-Semitic. In 1984, Farrakhan called Judaism a "dirty religion" and Hitler "wickedly great."[12] Said Farrakhan in one speech at Michigan State University, "You Jews suck the blood of the black community and you feel we have no right, now, to say something about it?"[13] Recently, in a section of Brooklyn, New York, the ill-feeling of blacks toward Jews turned violent after a black child was killed by an automobile driven by a Jew. Subsequently, a member of the Jewish Hasidic sect was stabbed to death during a racial melee.

On college campuses, too, places of supposedly enlightened thought, students make "hate speeches" or write racist articles for the campus press. Brown University recently expelled a student for shouting anti-Semitic, anti-black, and anti-homosexual slurs in a school courtyard. At Dartmouth College, the campus newspaper recently carried a quotation on its masthead from Hitler's autobiography. It read: "By warding off the Jews, I am fighting for the Lord's work." Worse, the quotation appeared on the first day of Yom Kippur, the most solemn Jewish holy day.

Anti-Semitism has even reared its head in countries where Jews and Judaism are hardly known. Japan is one. There are only a few hundred Jews living in Japan, and few if any of them have ever experienced any form of discrimination beyond the wariness that many Japanese, members of a society whose members are virtually all of the same stock, have of all foreigners. However, in the past few years, several hundred books on the Jews have appeared in Japan, some of them echoing the sentiments in the discredited Protocols of the Elders of Zion, that the Jews are attempting to control the world economy. (It is interesting to note that the same charge has been leveled against the Japanese by officials in the U.S., France, and elsewhere, a charge that the Japanese routinely dismiss as "Japan bashing.") One book popular in Japan denies that the Holocaust ever took place; another warns that Israel will start a third world war and shut off Japan's access to oil supplies in the Middle East. Once again, stereotypes are at work, repeating all the myths and misconceptions and feeding on people's fears.

Given all that we know about anti-Semitism, its prevalence and its roots, it would seem that abolishing it for good is an almost impossible task. There will always be people who never heed the message that all people are created equal, that prejudice, as the English essayist William Hazlitt described it, is the child of ignorance. There is little that one can do when dealing with someone who is a vocal anti-Semite except ignore him or her, or let them know you disagree or that you are offended by their views. Many psychologists and sociologists feel that instead of trying to change people's feelings, it is more effective to condemn the things that anti-Semites and other racists do and to condemn those acts loudly and clearly. If we discourage racist acts and let everyone know we will not tolerate them, there's a good chance they'll stop. We may not change a person's feelings, but they'll at least think twice about injuring someone, physically or emotionally, because of their religion or race. Discouraging anti-Semitism is something that all of us must do — you, your schools, our national leaders.

How you handle racism is, ultimately, up to you. If you are Jewish, you should make your feelings known to the offending person. If you are not, the same advice applies. If you have anti-Jewish feelings, try to put yourself in a Jew's mind. How would you like it if someone insulted your religion or ethnic background or told you that you ought to be barred from a club or a certain job because of your background? If you were a white living in Africa or a non-Asian living in China or Japan, chances are you'd understand fairly quickly what it's like to be "different." It's rather like making fun of someone's accent. You may think yours is normal but that of others is not — until the person you're mimicking tells you he or she thinks you sound strange, too.

Rarely does it do any good to simply ignore an anti-Semitic remark. For one thing, the person who makes the slur may be too stupid to realize that he or she has offended anyone and may well do it again because in the warped mind of a bigot, most everyone thinks the same way — the people the bigot hangs around with probably do. When a prejudiced person is hit with a strong reaction from a member of a group that he has insulted, or from a person who is not even a member of the group, the bigot has to notice, has to see that he or she is not in control. The bigot has to hear that he or she is out of line. Ignoring a racial insult will also only make the injured party feel more insecure about his or her background. Think of the times that you have been at a party or in your school lunchroom, maybe even at home, and someone made a nasty remark about Jews. Maybe it was a joke; maybe it was a critical comment about how Jews are too interested in money or too pushy; maybe it was just somebody saying, in a voice with a hard edge to it, "He's a Jew. Did you know that?" Now, if you're Jewish and you heard such a remark, did you leave the party or the cafeteria after expressing your feelings? Or did you just sit there and take it, but then fret about it for days?

For most of us, education is the best way to fight anti-Semitism and all other forms of prejudice. It can be fought, because hatred of others is not in our genes. We were not born with a gene coded for prejudice. We got our prejudices from a prejudiced environment, by conditioning. Unfortunately, the world is not prejudice free, and we cannot escape it. But prejudice can be prevented.

And the best prevention is information. The more information you have about the people you feel negatively about, the better you'll be able to understand them and, it is hoped, the easier you'll accept them. In the process, you might either see how much alike you are or how different you are. If you are convinced that we are all the same, under the skin, then you're on the right road. If you can understand and appreciate the differences between people, you're on the right road.

In the case of Jews, understand that each Jewish person is a unique mix of religion, culture, and national roots. Not all Jews are the same, just as not all Christians are the same, nor all blacks or Asians. The black Jews of Ethiopia, the Falasha, a people with a tradition that goes back to Biblical days, are as different from an American Jew as a German Christian is from a Native Brazilian who has been converted to Christianity.

From our discussion of race, you should understand that today's Jews are not a race in the usual sense of the word — that is, people of the same biological stock and physical type — but a diverse community, a fellowship, of people that has managed to maintain its identity through religious beliefs and customs ever since the Jewish nation was destroyed by the Romans.

"When you employ the term, 'Jewish,'" one observer wrote many years ago,

> you do not refer to a race but to an ancient religion, or to something which pertains to that ancient religion whose founders were the first to worship Jehova in a land of idolators, and whose moral precepts are a cornerstone of Christianity. . . . The Jewish people have never enjoyed the centuries of settled living in a single region which is required for the development of a distinct race. The original Jewish group was wholly a religious group. It drew converts from all of the races then living in the Near East. The big, high-bridged nose of the Near East was an Armenoid racial trait, characteristic of Hittites and ancient Greeks as well as of some Jews. The hooked nose was characteristic of certain groups within the Mediterranean race. Therefore, types often considered as "Jewish" are still

> common among non-Jews in the region from which the Jews originally came. Driven from one country to another for centuries, the Jews have long since lost any racial distinctions which they once possessed. In Europe and America they consequently reveal as much variation in physical type as do the gentile populations among whom they dwell.[14]

Anti-Semitism may well be with us for a long time, perhaps forever. Many members of Christian churches still find it difficult to accept Jews and the creation of the State of Israel. In fact, many Christians would not be unhappy if Israel's Arab neighbors overran the tiny country. Not because such Christians feel strongly for the Palestinians — whose anger at being displaced and left without a country of their own is not only understandable but justified — but because so many of them simply do not like Jews. Somebody always hates, often for very irrational reasons, and that is an unfortunate part of human nature. What we can hope for, however, is that the hatred be kept to a manageable minimum and that it never again explode into another Holocaust. We can also hope that ordinary people and national leaders, schools and businesses, the clergy and all the professions, will speak out against anti-Semitism at every opportunity and condemn in no uncertain terms those who preach and practice it. It is heartening to note that world leaders are doing just that. Russia, following suit to steps taken by the former Soviet Union, has been restoring religious liberties and has lightened its grip on the Jewish population. Another recent exemplary demonstration came in the spring of 1991 in Jerusalem. In a highly unusual and emotional speech before the Israeli Parliament, Polish president Lech Walesa apologized for his country's record of anti-Semitism. "Here in Israel, the land of your culture and revival," he told the assembly, which included survivors of the Nazi death camps in Poland, "I ask for your forgiveness. I am a Christian, and I cannot weigh with a human scale twenty centuries of evil for both of our people."[15]

Another moving demonstration occurred in Rome during a recent international conference on Catholic-Jewish relations. Pope John Paul II told the group about the close ties that Christianity has with Jews and Judaism and then closed his talk with a quotation from the Talmud. An observer at the scene noted that it was probably a first in papal history, since the Talmud had been burned by church authorities in the Middle Ages.[16]

If you are a Christian, you believe in Jesus Christ and that he shed his blood for all people. You believe that each one of us is made in his image. You should also know that your religion was born out of Judaism.

If you are a Muslim, you worship the one God of both Jews and Christians, and you know that your religion, Islam, means submission to God's will.

If you are a follower of Buddha, the prince who lived in India hundreds of years before Christ, you know that he taught universal brotherhood.

If you have no faith, and you are, as most people are, a good person, you probably automatically follow ordinary rules of behavior, some of which are based on religious principles. One good one is a precept first stated, in the days before Jesus, by a celebrated Jewish thinker named Hillel, when asked to sum up the teachings of Judaism: "What is hateful to you, do not do unto your neighbor."

5 • NATIVE AMERICANS
Maltreated Hosts

The only good Indians I ever saw were dead.
— General Philip Henry Sheridan

I am a representative of the original American race, the first people of this continent. We are good and not bad. The reports that you hear concerning us are all on one side.
— Red Cloud, Sioux Chief, 1870

The above remark by General Sheridan, one of the Union Army's most celebrated (and merciless) commanders during the Civil War, reflected an opinion held by many Americans back in the days of the Wild West. The Indians he spoke of were, of course, the Indians of North America, or more accurately, the Native Americans. Our Indians have been misnamed for centuries. When Columbus landed in Hispaniola in 1492, he mistakenly believed he had reached India. He called the unfamiliar people who lived there Indios. Later, others suggested that they should be called Amerindians, to identify them as early Americans, and to distinguish them from Indians from India. Actually, each tribe called itself by a name in its own language.

Despite many and continuing efforts to correct the mistake, *Indian* is still the mostly widely used term, and it is also used incorrectly to mean many different aboriginal peoples. But the wrong name Europeans gave the early inhabitants of North, Central, and South America is hardly the worst punishment that has been inflicted on them. If ever a group of people has been severely mistreated, misunderstood, and subjected to unrelenting prejudice, it is the Native Americans. They have been massacred, plundered, driven from their homes, resettled on reservations, and excluded from society. Impoverished, with their cultures destroyed and often forced to embrace a religion they did not understand or want, they became a forgotten minority.

Such harsh treatment obscures the rich culture and the many contributions and achievements of the Native Americans. They cultivated scores of crops — among them corn, tobacco, peanuts, beans, pumpkins, squash, and cotton. They knew how to irrigate their lands; fashion weapons and tools from flint, bronze, and stone; make jewelry and other ornaments from silver; and polish and mount precious stones. Indians wove baskets and cloth, built elaborate — and, in the case of the Incas, Aztecs, and Mayans, spectacular — temples, courtyards, and dwellings. They concocted potent and effective natural medicines, made swift canoes and sleds, and knew how to preserve meat and fish for the winter or for long journeys. Even in games and sports, Native Americans had much to give us — their game of lacrosse used a racquet not unlike the one we use today in tennis, and they also played dice and football and raced horses. They played drums, flutes, and whistles as well. Many of their songs and chants were beautiful, and so, too, were their dances. Native Americans also had great respect for nature, and they believed that every animal, plant, and rock had a spirit. They had their holy men and wise philosophers, brave warriors and able chiefs. And when the first colonists arrived, Native Americans offered them food and advice, not hostility.

"Civilized" white men — explorers, governors, missionaries — were responsible for the downfall of many primitive peoples, who were characterized as barbarians and savages. One wonders, however, just who were really the savages and who the civilized. The Spanish explorer Hernando de Soto, the first white man to see the Mississippi River, had a thirst for gold and land, and a cruel streak that he took out on the Native Americans of Florida every chance he could. Whenever de Soto and his men needed muscle, they chained packs of Indians together, beat them severely, and forced them to carry heavy supplies over miles of harsh, uncharted territory. Another vicious example is Francisco Pizarro, who landed near Peru in 1531, where a fabled people lived in beautiful cities and worshiped in magnificent temples filled with treasure. Pizarro knew that he could not conquer these hordes of natives with his relatively small army unless he captured their leader, who was known as the Inca. Pretending to be friendly, Pizarro invited the Inca to the Spanish camp. Almost immediately, the Inca's men were killed, and their leader thrown into a stone cell. In despair, the Inca told Pizarro that he would fill the cell with gold and jewels as high as a mark he had made on the wall if Pizarro would free him. Pizarro agreed, and the Inca made good on his promise. But Pizarro broke his end of the bargain. After collecting all the wealth, he had the Inca chained to a post to be burned to death. Bundles of wood were piled around the Inca, but for some reason, Pizarro changed his mind — not about killing the Inca, but about how. Instead of burning the Indians' chieftain, Pizarro ordered a cord knotted about the Inca's neck, and he was choked to death. Deprived of their leader, the native people surrendered, and Spain soon acquired a new colony.

Stories like this one abound in the history of the Native Americans. From the Inuit peoples in Alaska (also called Eskimos), who had to fend off white sealers, whalers, oil and gas prospectors, and fishermen; to the American Indians facing the early settlers who were after their land and bison; to the Yanomami of Brazil, who are even now threatened by gold miners carrying diseases against which the Yanomami have developed no resistance, aboriginal peoples have been sorely exploited.

Quite naturally, the Native Americans rebelled against the intrusions. Whites sometimes got back as much cruelty as they dispensed, and massacres of explorers and settlers were common in the early days. But while the killing of white settlers in the American West slowed expansion, it did not halt it. In 1830, President Andrew Jackson enforced a law that called for removing all Indian tribes east of the Mississippi River and resettling them in the West. More than 60,000 Indians were herded out, and those who refused were forced to march under such horrid conditions that of some 11,000 Cherokees moved, over 4,000 died.[1]

Few people could tell you much about those 4,000, as this incident has been left out of most American history textbooks. But just about everyone has learned about a much smaller number of victims of the U.S.–Indian conflict — the 250 U.S. cavalrymen who died at the Little Bighorn River near Hardin, Montana, in 1876. It was the site of the last stand of General George Armstrong Custer, whose men were surrounded by thousands of Native Americans led by Chief Sitting Bull and Chief Crazy Horse. While Custer and his men fought bravely, and deserve all the attention the incident has received in movies, books, and paintings, the other side of the story is that of the Indians: they never agreed that they were the aggressors. They argued that other calvary units provoked them by attacking Indian villages and that settlers had done the same by taking their land. Sitting Bull, who surrendered in 1881 and spent his last years on a reservation, summed up the Native Americans' position with these words:

> What treaty that the white man ever made with us have they kept? Not one. When I was a boy the Sioux owned the world; the sun rose and set on their land; they sent ten thousand men to battle. Where are the warriors today? Who slew them? Where are our lands? Who owns them? What law have I broken? Is it wrong for me to love my own? Is it wicked for me because my skin is red? Because I am a Sioux; because I was born where my father lived; because I would die for my people and my country?[2]

Sitting Bull's words would not be taken seriously. In 1890, during another outbreak involving the Sioux, he was killed near Fort Yates, North Dakota, allegedly while resisting arrest.

Two weeks after Sitting Bull's death, a number of Sioux fled a reservation in South Dakota. They were run down and rounded up by U.S. cavalrymen at Wounded Knee Creek. As the Sioux were being disarmed, a fight erupted, and the soldiers fired randomly, killing some two hundred. Historian Dee Brown has described the events of that day in his classic book, *Bury My Heart at Wounded Knee*:

> In the first seconds of violence, the firing of carbines was deafening, filling the air with powder smoke. . . . Then

> there was a brief lull in the rattle of arms, with small groups of Indians and soldiers grappling at close quarters, using knives, clubs, and pistols. As few of the Indians had arms, they soon had to flee, and then the big Hotchkiss guns on the hill opened up on them, firing almost a shell a second, raking the Indian camp, shredding the tepees with flying shrapnel, killing men, women, and children.
>
> "We tried to run," Louise Weasel Bear said, "but they shot us like we were buffalo. I know there are some good white people, but the soldiers must be mean to shoot children and women. Indian soldiers would not do that to white children."[3]

Wounded Knee is past, a dark part of history that some people try to forget, like the KKK lynchings in the South, the Holocaust, and the pogroms. But although the massacre at Wounded Knee occurred was many years ago, it would be wrong to forget it, just as it is wrong to forget the Holocaust and all of the other inhuman acts that have occurred throughout history. Wounded Knee is a symbol of what white Americans did to Americans who were "different." The plight of today's Native Americans — or what is left of that once-free group of people — is yet another reminder, a reprise, of the maltreatment their ancestors received here and in other countries.

Most of the two million Native Americans in the U.S. live today in what have been called "regions of refuge," places that are so remote and rugged that the industrial economy has avoided them. Moreover, millions of acres of ancestral land that are claimed by Indians are still controlled by whites. While large tracts of land have been transferred to Indians in the United States, according to Alan Thein Durning, who researches the relationships between social injustices and environmental issues at the Worldwatch Institute, Indian tribes have been pressing claims for some 35 million acres more of land for decades. Canada's backlog of claims is also large, says Durning, with indigenous groups demanding a third of the national territory. It is the same everywhere there are Indians. In Costa Rica, Indian lands are supposedly not for sale to non-Indians, but the reserves are full of non-Indian landowners who farm and ranch. As much as 70 percent of Mexico's forest land is theoretically under the control of indigenous and peasant communities, but state agencies responsible for managing natural resources rent most of the land to timber countries. In Brazil, mining concessions overlap 34 percent of Indian lands. A Colombian anthropologist quoted by Durning had this to say about the natives' desire to preserve what little they have:

> The Indians often tell me that the difference between a colonist and an Indian is that the colonist wants to leave money for his children and that the Indians want to leave forests for their children.[4]

What is life like on an Indian reservation? Here's how the American Indian Relief Council describes it:

- The highest teen suicide rate in America, triple the national average, is on Indian reservations.
- Per capita income is $1,238, about $100 a month for each man, woman and child.
- Only 10 percent of reservation families have telephones, and 70 percent have no access to a car.
- An Indian on the Rosebud Sioux reservation in South Dakota is ten times more likely to die by age forty-five than his counterpart in white America. The infant mortality rate there is double the national rate, and there is only one hospital — for a territory bigger than New York City and Long Island combined — with many Sioux living over 100 miles from the facility and the ambulance service.[5]

All this misery, even though our Indians were the first, and for a very long time, the foremost inhabitants of our continent. Would you like to live on a reservation? Probably not. Would you like to have your family, which is what the Native American tribes are, abolished, as was done in the 1950s as part of a U.S. government policy known as termination? That policy took away tribal lands and the Indians' identities in return for cash payments. The goal was to get Native Americans to assimilate. Congress eventually reversed this decision and officially recognized the individual tribes, and Native Americans have tried to rebuild their nations, sometimes without land, never with much more than a relatively small piece. As one tribal leader once put it, "We started out with millions of acres, and we're down to a cemetery."

Long ago, two famous Indian leaders, Red Jacket and Tecumseh, addressed the white men who had tried to wipe America clean of the tribes. Unfortunately, they have not gotten the same attention moviemakers and novelists paid to the exploits of the Apache raiders, Cochise and Geronimo, and to one of the Sioux leaders at the Battle of Little Bighorn, Crazy Horse. But their words bear listening to today, when prejudice and discrimination are so rampant in our society.

Red Jacket, born near Geneva, New York, was a chief of the Senecas and a skilled orator. In 1805, he spoke at a meeting of chiefs, but he directed his remarks to a white missionary who was in attendance. This is part of what Red Jacket said:

> Brother, listen to what we say. There was a time when our forefathers owned this great island. Their seats extended from the rising to the setting sun. The Great Spirit had made it for the use of Indians. . . .
>
> But an evil day came upon us. Your forefathers crossed the great water and landed on this island. Their numbers were small. They found friends and not enemies. They told us they had fled from their own country for fear of wicked men and had come here to enjoy their religion. They asked us for a small seat. We took pity on them, granted their request, and they sat down among us. We gave them corn and meat. They gave us poison in return. . . .
>
> Brother, continue to listen. . . . You have got your country but you are not satisfied. You want to force your religion upon us. . . . You say you are right and we are lost. . . . But we also have a religion which was given to our forefathers and has been handed down to us. We worship in that way. It teaches us to be thankful for all the favors we receive, to love each other, and to be united. . . .
>
> Brother, the Great Spirit has made us all, but He has made a great difference between His white and His red

> children. He has given us different complexions and different customs. . . . Why may we not conclude that He has given us a different religion according to our understanding? The Great Spirit does right. He knows what is best for His children. We are satisfied.[6]

In 1810, Tecumseh, a Shawnee chief from Ohio, directed the following remarks to William Henry Harrison, who was governor of Indiana at the time and had just negotiated large purchases of Indian lands:

> Once [we were] a happy race, since made miserable by the white people, who are never contented, but always encroaching. The way, and the only way, to check and to stop this evil, is for all the red men to unite in claiming a common and equal right in the land, as it was at first, and should be yet; for it never was divided, but belongs to all for the use of each. That no part has a right to sell, even to each other, much less to strangers, those who want all and will not do with less. The white people have no right to take the land from the Indians because they had it first; it is theirs.[7]

Three years later, Tecumseh was killed in the Battle of the Thames in Canada while fighting with the British against the United States in the War of 1812. The leader of the victorious Americans in the Battle of the Thames was William Henry Harrison, by then a general in the army. In 1840, Harrison was elected the ninth president of the United States. He died of pneumonia after only a month in office, but he had silenced a "troublemaking Indian" and had helped solidify America's claims to Native American territory.

It is doubtful that the nation's Native Americans will ever have their original holdings restored — the U.S. isn't about to "give it all back to the Indians." But we can let them have their dignity, their rights, their identity. It is the least we can do for our original Americans. And perhaps if we think every so often about how the Native Americans have been mistreated, it will help us to speak out against mindless prejudice whenever this poison is sprayed at other groups of people.

6 • IMMIGRANTS
Strength in Diversity

Give me your tired, your poor
Your huddled masses yearning to breathe free,
The wretched refuse of your teeming shore,
Send these, the homeless, tempest-tossed to me:
I lift my lamp beside the golden door.
— Emma Lazarus, Inscription at the base of the Statue of Liberty

E pluribus unum.
(One out of many.)
— Used on the seal of the United States

Each and every one of us, with the sole exception of full-blooded Native Americans, is descended from immigrants, people who came to this country from somewhere else to make a permanent home. Most immigrants came freely in search of a better life, usually with little or no money but with a lot of hopes and dreams. Many Africans came against their will aboard slave ships, and it would be many years before they would be as free as all the other immigrants. Still others came in "without papers," sneaking across our borders on foot, stowed away on ocean liners, or sailing in on small boats.

They still come — some 700,000 a year legally. Thousands more come here illegally, from Ireland, Mexico, and other countries. Or they flee from a military takeover on the Caribbean island of Haiti, try to enter the United States, and are kept aboard Coast Guard vessels until their plight can be resolved. Legal or illegal, immigrants were our past and are our future. Each group contributes something valuable to our society, and no single group can be considered better than any other.

The English and the Dutch were among the first to settle here from abroad, and they soon took charge. The English established the first permanent settlement in America in Jamestown, Virginia, in 1607; thirteen years later, the English also colonized Plymouth, Massachusetts, arriving aboard the *Mayflower* after fleeing religious persecution at home. Dutch settlers planted their flag near the Hudson River in 1624, a location that became New York forty years afterward. Most people are probably unaware that around the time of the American Revolution, Dutch was a major language in New York and New Jersey.

But it was the English who were to dominate early America for years to come. Fiercely loyal to the British crown and proud of their British ancestry, these early immigrants controlled government, education, religion, trade, and just about every activity in the daily lives of everyone who lived in what was appropriately named New England. Later, it was those with the same English roots who fought against the English king in the American Revolution and drew up the Declaration of Independence and the Constitution to give birth to the America we know today. To immigrants, then, we owe our nation.

As the years passed and America expanded, the nation's reputation overseas as a land of equal opportunity for all grew. More and more newcomers came, not all from the "Mother Country," as England was affectionately known, but from the "Old Country" as well, continental Europe.

In the hundred years between 1830 and 1930, some 40 million people migrated to the United States. The migration reached its height in the early twentieth century, when more than a million entered the country every year. Up until 1850, immigration was mainly from Great Britain, Ireland, Germany, Norway, Sweden, and Denmark. Later, immigrants from those countries made up a smaller percentage of the arrivals and were replaced by people from Italy, Russia, and other countries in southern and eastern Europe.

Ellis Island, just a few hundred yards from the Statue of Liberty in New York Harbor, was the major federal immigration facility in America. Between 1891, the year it was opened, and 1954, the year it was closed as an active receiving station, 12 million immigrants were processed there, more than 11,000 on one record day in 1907.

What was it like, coming to a new country? This is how an immigrant from Europe recalled the experience:

> I will never forget the joy I felt when I saw the tall buildings of New York and the Statue of Liberty after so many dark days on board that crowded ship. There was the symbol of all my dreams — freedom to start out in a new life. Then came Ellis Island. It was called by us the Island of Tears. In my village, I had heard of this place to be inspected and maybe, it was said, sent home if you did not pass. Sent home to what? I worried. I tried to convince myself that America would never send me home once I had reached her doors. When I landed the noise and commotion were unbelievable. There were so many languages being spoken. The shouting and pushing guards calling out the big numbers on the tags attached to our coats created more noise and confusion. Surely, I felt, the noise surrounding the Tower of Babel could not have been worse.
>
> We were told to keep moving and to hurry up as my group was pushed along one of the dozens of metal railings that divided the room into several passageways. Immigrants walked along these passageways until they reached the first medical inspector who looked at face, hair, neck and hands. Interpreters asked, "What is your age?" "What work do you do?"
>
> I walked on to where a doctor inspected me for diseases. . . . I passed inspection but the man in front was marked with an "E" in chalk on his coat and sent to another area. I had heard that an "E" meant deportation.
>
> Finally, I went before a tired, stern-looking official who checked my name against the ship's passenger list and quickly fired questions at me: "Can you read and write?" "Do you have a job waiting for you?" "Who paid for your passage?" "Have you ever been in prison?" "How much money do you have?" "Let me see it now."
>
> Suddenly, I was handed a landing card. It was hard to

> believe the ordeal was over. The fears I had earlier were unfounded. The statue in the harbor had not turned her back on me. America had accepted me.[1]

Today, more than 40 percent of all living Americans, over 100 million people, can trace their roots to an ancestor who came into the United States through Ellis Island. More immigrants poured into the country through other ports, and they continue to arrive to this day.

Life was supposed to be better here than in the countries the immigrants left behind. For some it was, and for others it wasn't. Some of the earlier immigrants — among them the Germans, Norwegians, Swedes, and French — arrived with a little money, and many were artisans; these people moved west and established farms or pursued a number of crafts and businesses. Many became as successful and as influential as the descendants of the English, and because the areas they settled were more open and had a less diverse ethnic population, life there, though often full of hardships, was not as cruel as it was in the big cities.

Most of the immigrants, however, had to stick it out in the crowded, multiethnic port cities where they landed. They couldn't afford to move away, and most were uneducated. The men were generally unskilled laborers. Few spoke English. Their "strange" customs and behavior also set them apart. They found work, but the conditions were terrible; many who came from rural, naturally beautiful regions regretted that they had left. They were paid for their labors, but it was a starvation wage. They had places to live, but they were usually filthy, unheated, unventilated rooms in tenements in the worst sections of town or tents in squatters' parks. There was food, but it was simple, and there was never enough. They did not have Indians and droughts and tornadoes to contend with, as the settlers in the West did, but there was plenty of street crime, hunger, and disease.

For many years, the immigrant experience was more painful than comfortable, more captive than free. Often, it was only the newcomers' muscle and brawn that were appreciated. Sadly, even though the founding fathers dreamed of a nation made up of many different peoples and the Declaration of Independence declared all men to be equal, the new immigrants too often became second-class citizens in the New World because the unofficial rule was that those who were here first got the best deal.

The more wealthy and educated sons and grandsons of the early English settlers held firm control for many years. Many Protestants looked down on the "foreigners," many of whom now were Catholics or Jews, even though they themselves had either come from overseas or were descended from parents who had. Even the lower-class Yankees felt they were worth more than the newcomers, but most times, the only advantage they had was not intelligence or any special skill but the English language, which enabled them to get by far easier than those who could speak only Italian, German, Yiddish, or Polish. The immigrants from Europe were often quite aware of that irony. As some used to say about the *Mayflower* descendants, "Don't forget — they came over on a cattle boat, too." Or, as one standard joke among the Irish had it, "Those people on the *Mayflower* were just the servants sent over to ready the summer cottages for their masters."

Eventually another revolution would occur — a peaceful one this time, against the English who were now Americans and who wielded the power as though they were the only Americans. It would take a while, but the newcomers would acquire enough solidarity and strength to gain a measure of respect, to win a share of the power, and, in some places, even take it away.

As the ethnic groups fought their way into the higher places in the political and social systems, they rarely did it together — at least not at the outset. *Unum* was more important than *pluribus* for the new immigrants, and so each group carved out its own power base and took care of its own. And as it was with the Yankees against the people from the Old Country, so it became with one ethnic group against another.

The reasons that immigrants suffer discrimination today are the same as always, ranging from fear that "foreigners" are taking jobs from "real Americans" to fear that they will "pollute" the dominant culture to stereotypic views of how certain groups behave and think. As New York Governor Mario Cuomo has said, "Distinct ethnic types are always threatening to somebody."[2] Perhaps that is why we have had so many quotas over the years, limitations on how many of each ethnic group are allowed to enter the United States. Sometimes restriction acts were imposed because economic conditions had caused high unemployment and the government wanted the available jobs to go to those already living here; other times, quota laws were driven by outright bias and were passed to keep out certain ethnic groups, as well as those "morally or physically undesirable." Sometimes, too, the immigration laws gave preference to aliens with special skills or trades, discriminating against the unschooled and untrained. And sometimes violence was used to discourage immigrants. In the 1850s, the Native American Party, popularly known as the Know-Nothings, tried to stop foreigners and Roman Catholics from winning public office. The Know-Nothings assaulted Catholics and immigrants on the streets and in their homes, sometimes with deadly results.

Unfortunately, distrust of someone who is different seems to be part of human nature. Being different can be a valuable trait, but it can also be a heavy burden. Generations of immigrants have had to deal with the challenges of being a foreigner in the United States, with both the advantages of working in a new country and the disadvantages. One Pakistani who came to Washington, D.C., not so long ago drove a cab for a time and now owns five taxi companies; he has expressed the bittersweet experience of being an immigrant: "We came here because of the opportunities. If there is any discrimination, that's part of the deal. I have learned to live with it. Individuals may treat you badly, but basically the system is fair."[3]

We cannot do justice to all of our immigrant groups in a book of this kind, and we apologize to those who have been excluded. So many have come, from the world's major countries to the tiniest islands. Hundreds of languages, from Arabic to Zapotec, are spoken here. There are even sections in some of our cities where it is not uncommon to see a sign in a store that proclaims reassuringly — for the benefit of the minority who now live in the neighborhood — "English Spoken Here." The best we can do is look at the immigrant populations that came in great waves to America, at the obstacles they had to overcome as they tried to become Americans, and at the prejudices they encountered because they were "different." We have elected to discuss the experiences of the African-Americans and the Jews in separate chapters. Those we look at now in capsule form are not only among the most visible of the other immigrants, but they are also representative of all who have come here because their trials and experiences are shared by every immigrant.

THE IRISH

The Irish were among our earliest immigrants, but it was a potato blight in 1845 that turned their migration into a flood. Deprived of one of their most precious staples and faced with unbearable famine that lasted several years and killed about a million people, they fled to America by the hundreds of thousands. Most were peasants — and illiterate because up until 1831, their Protestant British rulers had prohibited Irish Catholics from going to school. The few who had any education had acquired it since 1831, or earlier from teachers who had conducted secret classes in the woods and in farmhouses. Irish Catholics had also been forbidden to own land and had been forced to pay tithes to the Anglican church.

When the Irish arrived here, they settled in the big cities of the northeast, the men working on construction jobs — the major railroads and canals across the country were built mostly by Irish, and Chinese, laborers — the women as servants in the homes of the wealthy. The men's wages were around 50 cents a day (the women received less), but there was always the promise, as expressed in a popular expression of the time, of "A dollar a day, the white man's pay." Sometimes, though, finding a job or a place to live was difficult, unless one had helpful friends or relatives who had come over earlier. It was not uncommon to see signs proclaiming, "No Irish Need Apply," posted in tenements and on job sites.

Vilified and mistrusted by the Protestant English who were now their masters again, the Irish were derided as "the scum of creation," as muckers, greenhorns, micks, and Paddies. They were stereotyped as drunkards, thugs, dirty, and pig-headed. They were accused of refusing to become "real Americans," of being clannish and of clinging to customs that were perceived as being born of ignorance and superstition. Their church, which had become an Irish fortress surrounded by hostile forces, was feared and hated. Their large families were seen as a threat.

Some of the animosity grew out of the fact that the Irish did commit a high proportion of the crimes during the early years, and they were poorer than the rest of the population. But their poverty and criminal activity were the result of environmental influences imposed on them by the very people who frowned on them. Over the years, to keep out these "undesirables," Irish immigration would be severely restricted.

The Irish soon began to stand up for themselves, however. Former peasants soon became streetwise, outspoken, and politically active in Democratic politics. They argued forcefully against the Protestant version of the Bible and the Protestant textbooks used to instruct Irish children in the public schools. Kept out of big-city politics for years, they began intimidating non-Democrats who tried to vote Republican in Irish districts. "Where the Irish had been wild, they now became tough," wrote Senator Daniel Patrick Moynihan. "Where they had been rebellious, it now became more a matter of being defiantly democratic."[4] And for some Irishmen, being defiantly democratic meant not only intimidating Republican voters but sometimes assaulting them. In one bloody confrontation in Philadelphia, a Protestant youth was killed. In retaliation, "American Republicans" attacked and burned down thirty houses and two churches in an Irish neighborhood; hundreds of Irish families were left homeless, and in the riots that followed, more than thirty people were killed.

By 1870, there were nearly a half-million foreign-born people in New York City, some 40 percent of them Irish. In 1880, the city elected its first Catholic mayor, William R. Grace, the founder of a huge shipping line. Irish-Americans now ran the governments of many large cities, controlled city jobs, and made up most of the police and fire departments. Once victims of prejudice, the Irish were now running things.

Unfortunately, like virtually all immigrants and their descendants, many of the Irish developed deep prejudices of their own. Most people, as we have said, are frightened and threatened by aliens, by anyone who is different. Many of the Irish were no exception. For all that they had had to take from their English overseers, one would think they could sympathize with newly arrived immigrants from other cultures, people who had to go through just what they themselves had. But that is too simple a conclusion. For many, fear of being shut out again, of having to give up the power and jobs they had fought so long for, overrode any sentiments about justice and a share of the pie for all. Too often, fair play and the notion that all men are created equal are okay as long as it doesn't mean giving anything up.

As it can do to anyone, too much power made some Irish-American politicians arrogant. Irish politics became synonymous with corruption and scandalous behavior. Tammany Hall, headquarters of the Irish-dominated political organization in New York City, was the headquarters of that corruption. Tammany's bosses issued the orders for municipal control, and its members did their best to keep other ethnic groups out of City Hall. "They had good teachers," was how one Yankee politician, now stripped of all influence, would put it ruefully. "Us."

In the mid-1800s, a group of Irish-American coal miners formed a secret society called the Molly Maguires. It was modeled on a terrorist group in Ireland whose name came from the female disguises its members wore. The original Molly Maguires believed that the only way to right the many injustices that had been inflicted upon them by landlords and English laws was physical violence against the oppressors. The American Mollies operated in the mining district of Pennsylvania. There, Irish-American laborers faced many of the same injustices that the Irish in Ireland had faced. Miners worked under harsh conditions, and mine operators controlled virtually every aspect of their lives: the workers lived in company-owned dormitories and were paid in company-issued "money," called scrip, which they could use only at company-owned stores. Aware that the Molly Maguires in Ireland had solved some of the peasants' economic and political troubles, the American Mollies decided that terrorism was the only way that Irish-Americans in Pennsylvania could improve their situation. The Mollies started strikes, and they also launched murderous attacks on mine owners and agents. In 1876, several of the organizations' leaders were arrested, convicted, and hanged.

During the Civil War, some Irish-Americans supported the Union cause: 150,000 Irish-born Americans — not counting second- and third-generation Irish-Americans — fought in the Union army. But some Irish-Americans were upset at what they felt was a war conducted by the Protestant Englishmen they hated so much for the benefit of another group they despised, the blacks who were demanding freedom. The hostility of some toward those who backed the Union cause in the war exploded in riots in July of 1863 in New York City. Known as the draft riots, they began as a protest against a government policy that allowed people with money to either hire someone to serve in the Army in their place or to buy an exemption for $300. At first, the predominantly Irish-American mobs that gathered to protest the unfair law directed their anger against the draft offices, attacking and burning them down. Then the violent behavior escalated, as it so often does. The targets now became blacks, who, in the eyes of the protesters, were not only taking laborers' jobs away from them in the city but were the real cause of the war, which was unpopular with some.

Gangs of Irishmen assaulted blacks on the streets and performed several lynchings. Negro homes, an orphanage for black children, and the homes of abolitionists were sacked and burned; several Protestant churches were also burned, and a good deal of industrial machinery that helped automate factories was destroyed. Well-dressed whites were also assaulted on sight on the assumption that they were war sympathizers and "naygur lovers." U.S. Marines, the state militia, and New York City police finally put down the rioting, but not before 1,000 people had been killed, most of them blacks and other civilians. The draft riots were among the worst in American history and stand as a graphic example of prejudice run amok.

But despite the outrages some Irish-Americans committed and despite the outrages committed against them, the Irish immigrants prospered, and many have contributed mightily to America and the rest of the world. From poet William Butler Yeats to politician John Fitzgerald Kennedy, from dramatist George Bernard Shaw to cardinals of the Catholic church, from Irish nannies to Irish minstrels, Ireland has produced, in every conceivable occupation, an array of movers and shakers that shatters the bigoted view that all Irish are brawlers who can never become respectable. When President Kennedy's father, Joseph — the son of an Irish immigrant who had settled in Boston — was appointed ambassador to Great Britain by President Franklin D. Roosevelt, his comment to his wife, Rose, typified the pride of the Irish who had been kept down for so many centuries by the English. "Well, Rose," he said while on their way to dinner with the king and queen at Windsor Castle, "this is a helluva long way from East Boston, isn't it?"[5] On the day President Kennedy died, the Speaker of the U.S. House of Representatives, the Senate Majority Leader, and the chairman of the Democratic National Committee were all Catholic Irish-Americans.

Some sociologists argue that the Irish in America have "quit being Irish," that is, they have assimilated too much, that the breed of Irish-Americans who created powerful political and church bases are dying out and that Irish influence is dead or dying. That is debatable.

One reason the Irish in America will probably never quit being Irish is new immigration. America's place in the world as a haven and, in good times, a place of incomparable opportunity, is not likely to change. For the Irish, who have historically been a key part of America's immigrant residents, a new provision in the immigration laws will continue that tradition: over the next few years, under an annual lottery system that grants permanent residency to "winners" from thirty-four countries, Irish immigrants will be favored with 40 percent of the available places. That means that thousands of Irish will be coming to America every year. Opponents of the lottery argue that it favors white Europeans and emphasizes national origins and a quota system that was dropped in 1965. Proponents like Senator Edward M. Kennedy have answered the criticism by saying that the lottery simply rights years of discrimination against Irish immigrants who were limited to fewer than 1,000 visas a year.

There is another reason why Irish influence in America is unlikely to wither. Second-, third-, and fourth-generation Irish may well forget some of the old ways of their immigrant ancestors, and it is doubtful than any Americanized Irish would ever want to live as the immigrants did. But being Irish-American, like being of any ethnic descent, is not a suit or a dress that can or should be discarded at will. An Irisher can change his or her name or religion but cannot forget Irish history, nor the traditions of his or her ancestors. Our ethnic heritage is like a ghost that does not rest.

THE ITALIANS

Long before Italian immigrants began flocking to America in the late 1800s, Italians had visited our shores, playing a vital role in the European exploration of the Americas and the island countries that lie off America. The exploits of Christopher Columbus in our offshore waters are well known, but others landed on the American continent and paved the way for later British settlements and claims. Giovanni da Verrazzano led an expedition for the French into what would be known centuries later as New York Harbor and explored the eastern coast of the United States, making numerous landings on American soil from Florida to Maine in the 1500s. Verrazzano was the first explorer to describe accurately the landmarks he surveyed. The new land was named America after Amerigo Vespucci, a Florentine navigator who also explored the New World. Had it not been for Vespucci, we might be known today as Francescans, after the name Francesca, which Verrazzano gave to the lands he discovered.[6] Two more important Italian explorers were Giovanni Caboto, known by his English name John Cabot, and his son Sebastian, both of whom sailed for the British. Soon after Columbus's voyages, John explored the northern part of North America and was the first European to see Newfoundland; Sebastian explored South America.

Italians were also influential during colonial days, and several fought for General Washington in the revolution. Cosimo dei Medici distinguished himself at the battle of Brandywine Creek and was instrumental in creating the U.S. Cavalry. Onorio Razzolini of Maryland was probably the first Italian to hold public office in the new nation when he was named armourer and keeper of stores. William Paca, a governor of Maryland, was of Italian origin and a signer of the Declaration of Independence. The preamble to that historic document contains words remarkably similar to those written in Italian two years earlier by Thomas Jefferson's close friend Filippo Mazzei:

> All men are by nature created free and independent. Such equality is necessary in order to create a free government. It is necessary that all men be equal to each other in natural law. A true republican government cannot exist unless men from the richest to the poorest are perfectly equal in their natural rights.[7]

Many years later, when Italians began pouring into America, contributions like those of Mazzei and the others who had played parts in the development of the new nation were all but forgotten, buried under the weight of prejudice. In his concern over the passing of the "great race," Madison Grant typified the opinion Americans generally held about the largely illiterate Italians who had arrived in search of a dream. To Grant, anyone who came from the Mediterranean regions was inferior and vulgar, and literally the "wretched refuse" from teeming shores, which was hardly what Emma Lazarus meant when she wrote her inscription for the Statue of Liberty.

Italians entering the New World settled mostly in dingy city tenements and worked as day laborers or opened barbershops and shoe repair shops. All had a rough time of it — sometimes worse than earlier immigrants because they could not speak English and their culture was quite unlike that of the English and the Irish. Many Protestant English regarded Italians as uncouth and crime-prone; many Irish saw them as threats in the job market and didn't appreciate the Italian's looser, "saints-and-festivals" brand of Catholicism. Some Irish-American priests even went so far as to refer disparagingly to Italians as "dagoes" from the pulpit and forced them to sit in the back of churches with blacks.[8] The press was no better. One newspaper had this to say in 1900 about the European immigrants, most of them Italians and Jews:

> The floodgates are open. The dam is washed away. The sewer is choked. Europe is vomiting! The scum of immigration is viscerating upon our shores. The horde of $9.60 steerage slime [steerage is the section of a passenger ship

> with the lowest fares and the worst living conditions] is being siphoned upon us from continental mud tanks.[9]

Italian immigrants also suffered at the hands of their own kind, the padroni. *Padroni* is Italian for patrons or protectors, but the padroni, Italians who had been in America for some time and had learned how to exploit people and the American system, were hardly benevolent. The padroni became unofficial bankers, loaning money at high interest to Italian immigrants; they also secured jobs for recent immigrants and supposedly acted as middlemen between workers and employers. But the padroni took every advantage they could of the ignorant peasants who, for the most part, were digging ditches and subways with picks and shovels, living in shanties and boxcars, and earning $1.50 a day for twelve hours a day of backbreaking, often dangerous, labor.

Swindled, threatened, and sometimes murdered by their own countrymen, discriminated against by their employers, lacking political clout, and shut out by the predominantly Irish Catholic church, many Italians lost hope and returned to Italy. Another blow would shut them out in another way: in 1917, Congress passed a law requiring immigrants to be literate, which effectively prevented Italians from southern Italy, the poorest region of Italy, from coming over. A subsequent quota system also severely limited the number of Italian immigrants, and it remained in effect until 1965, when President Johnson abolished it.

Italians in America also had to fight off two stereotypes that plagued them at every turn: that they were all criminals or anarchists. The first one still dogs Italians and their descendants. It is true that Sicilians brought the crime organization, the Mafia, to America, and made it a terrifying force in the 1800s, and it is also true that organized criminal gangs of Italian-Americans patterned after the Sicilian Mafia exist today. The Mafia "offered" protection to merchants, loaned money through a loan-shark system, ran gambling and prostitution rings, controlled businesses and, eventually, when the Italians acquired political power, politics as well. Italian gangsters — Charles ("Lucky") Luciano and Al ("Scarface") Capone among them — were household names during the Prohibition period, in the 1920s, when liquor was illegal but when racketeers managed to keep supplying people who wanted to drink.

It should be obvious that not all Italian-Americans were criminals in those violent times, no more than they are today. Unfortunately, however, the actions of a fairly large number of gangsters with Italian names and the willingness of people to accept stereotypes clouded a lot of minds. On March 14, 1891, an incident occurred in New Orleans that underscores the mindless nature of prejudice.

It began with the murder of Police Chief David Hennessy, who, before he died, muttered, "The dagoes did it." Goaded by the press and a hostile public, police rounded up more than a hundred Italian-Americans. Nine were put on trial, but because there was no evidence to prove they had committed the crime, none were convicted. Soon after, a mob led by a young man named William Parkerson stormed the jail where the suspects were being held. Two of the suspects were hanged, and nine others were shot to death.

In an interview with a newspaper reporter, Parkerson showed no remorse for his role in the vigilante attack, characterizing it as a public service. "We had a thirty-minute experience that Saturday," he said with a smile. "The most wonderful thing about it is that it was over so soon. I take more credit for that than anything else." Asked how he felt about a mob killing defenseless men, Parkerson replied, "Of course, it is not a courageous thing to attack a man who is not armed, but we looked upon these as so many reptiles."[10]

The incident touched off an international cry of outrage, and for a while diplomatic relations between Italy and the U.S. were broken. But it would not be the last such attack against Italian-Americans. One case in Massachusetts that also riveted the world's attention was fueled not only by the general belief that Italians were a violent people but also by the view that they were anarchists, people who believe that all forms of government are unnecessary and undesirable.

The case involved Nicola Sacco, a shoemaker, and Bartolomeo Vanzetti, a fish peddler, who were charged with murdering a paymaster and a guard at a Braintree, Massachusetts, shoe factory during a robbery in 1920. During Sacco and Vanzetti's two-month trial, the prosecution relied heavily on often questionable eyewitness evidence and made much of the defendants' anarchistic views and activities and the fact that they had avoided military service during World War I. The emphasis on the defendants' politics was perhaps influenced by the fact that many Italians in Italy, and some in America, did indeed harbor a strong distaste for state authority and had become revolutionaries. Some twenty years before Sacco and Vanzetti went to trial, an Italian anarchist had murdered the Empress of Austria-Hungary, and another Italian who was living in New Jersey went back to Italy to assassinate King Umberto I.

With a fear of anarchists uppermost in their minds, the prosecution, the judge, the jury, and even the governor of the state seemed bent on punishing the men for their political beliefs and for being draft dodgers rather than for the murders. The judge, Webster Thayer, even remarked outside the courtroom during the trial that he would "get those anarchist bastards."[11] One of the jurors used the term "dagoes," a reflection of the strong anti-Italian sentiments being expressed at the time. In such a climate of prejudice, Sacco and Vanzetti were found guilty by the jury after only five hours of deliberation and were sentenced to death. "I am suffering because I am a radical," Vanzetti said bitterly, "and indeed I am a radical. I have suffered because I was an Italian, and indeed I am an Italian."

Later, a man who was in prison for another murder confessed that he had participated in the Braintree crime and that Sacco and Vanzetti were innocent. More than a dozen Italian-Americans swore under oath that the two men were miles from the scene of the crime at the time it was committed. A scientist provided photographs showing that the bullet that killed the guard could not have come from Sacco's gun. Famed Harvard law professor Felix Frankfurter, who would later become a justice of the U.S. Supreme Court, published a review of the case that exonerated the defendants and called special attention to Judge Thayer's bias during the trial. The defense asked for a retrial, but it was denied.

Finally, the defense took the case to the governor, who appointed a committee — whose members included the presidents of Harvard University and the Massachusetts Institute of Technology — to study the case. In August of 1927, the governor concluded that Sacco and Vanzetti had received a fair trial and that they were guilty. Riots and protests erupted in a number of cities; bombs went off in subways, in churches, and at the homes of jurors. The demonstrations spread to foreign countries, but they were to no avail. Sacco and Vanzetti were placed in stifling lightproof and soundproof cells to await their executions. "Just think of it!" wrote Vanzetti. "They have persecuted us to death for seven long years . . . and they have transferred us here, just to deprive us for a month of a little fresh air and sunlight, of some visits; just to inflict upon us thirty days more of solitary confinement, at the hottest of the summer, in a low, smoky, dreadful place before they burn us to death. And this is enlightened America."[12] On August 23, 1927, Sacco and Vanzetti, along with the man who said he had participated in the crime, went to the electric chair.

The case is still debated today, but the evidence is quite strong that the two immigrants were innocent of the Braintree murder.

Gradually, Italians in America overcame much of the prejudice. Slow to take advantage of their unifying Catholicism and of the political and educational systems — the old-timers had a distrust of the church, of strong government, and of education, institutions that they associated with exploitive priests, politicians, and professors — Italians finally saw the need to do what the Irish had done before them. They learned politics from the Irish, and sometimes even changed their names to ease the way into the system. In New York City, Antonio Maggio, a politician and successful banker, went by the name James March; Paolo Antonio Vaccarelli, vice president of the Longshoreman's Union and a Tammany Hall political activist, was known as Paul Kelley.

The Catholic church, too, became a source of strength for the Italians. In 1888, the Missionary Society of the Fathers of Saint Charles (known as the Scalabrini Fathers) came to New York City and Boston to take care of the immigrants' spiritual needs, to help them find jobs and medical care, and to set up homes for the aged, social centers, and a system of parochial schools. Without the priests and brothers, many thousand Italian immigrants in every major city of the United States would not only have drifted away from their faith but "would have easily become people without the solid roots that now enable them to make important contributions of their genius and customs to the growth and development of this country."[13]

A list of all the Italian immigrants and their descendants who have left their mark on America, and in some instances the world, is not possible here. Filippo Mazzei and William Paca made their contributions during colonial days. In more modern times we can point to Saint Frances Xavier Cabrini (Mother Cabrini), the first canonized American citizen; the Nobel Prize–winning physicist Enrico Fermi, whose intensive scrutiny of the properties of gases, metals, and subatomic particles helped usher in the age of nuclear energy; to Joe DiMaggio, the famed New York Yankees slugger whose as yet unbeaten hitting streak made him a member of the baseball Hall of Fame; to Salvatore Lombino, who writes novels under the names Evan Hunter and Ed McBain; to Academy Award–winning actors Robert DeNiro and Joe Pesci; to politician Geraldine Ferraro; to Lee Iacocca, who headed the giant automaker Chrysler. Each has, in his or her own way, demonstrated the worthlessness of stereotypes and the gross unfairness of prejudice.

THE ASIANS

Asia is an enormous continent, the world's largest. Its islands and countries stretch from the Arctic Circle to the Equator, and its distance from east to west is more than twice that across the United States.

Over the years, immigrants have come to America from many of the countries and regions that make up Asia: India, China, Japan, Taiwan, the Philippines, Korea, Vietnam, Cambodia, Laos, and various Pacific islands. In the early nineteenth century, most of the immigrants were from China and Japan. Most came here to escape economic hardships, as did most other immigrants and, in the case of the Chinese, to seek fortunes in the gold mines of California before returning home. But later, an increasing number of Asian immigrants came from other countries in the region, and many of them were refugees from political turmoil and persecution at home. After the Vietnam War, for instance, America welcomed Vietnamese refugees who fled the communist takeover of the country, along with Cambodians who escaped from the Khmer Rouge, the rebel group that conquered Cambodia and massacred the population in one of history's worst cases of genocide.

In 1965, the Asian-American population in the United States numbered about a million, and in 1980 around three million. Today, it is more than seven million — about half immigrants, the others children born here of Asian parents who were immigrants — making them the country's fastest-growing minority.

All Asian groups that have come here have been the targets of mindless bigotry. Their vastly different cultures, with their unfamiliar religions and seemingly "incomprehensible" languages, set them apart from the European-descended, Christian American majority. But when America was new, they were welcomed for a time because they were willing to work incredibly hard for cheap wages, and there was plenty of work involved in building the new nation. The Asians, thus, soon became a labor problem as much as a cultural one because their willingness and ability to get by on next to nothing were threatening to American workers who were looking for better wages. The fact that many Asians were and still are frugal, able to save even from skimpy wages, is a virtue that does not always set well with those who waste and indulge themselves and are threatened by competition. We tend not to like people who show us up.

With the understanding that all Asian-Americans live in an alien world in the U.S. — like African-Americans, who cannot escape their color, Asians cannot escape the fact that they will always stand out because they cannot hide the shape of their eyes — and that all have suffered from time to time at the hands of bigots, we will focus here on only two groups, the Chinese and Japanese, who were exposed for a long time to some special brands of prejudice and discrimination that deserve attention.

First, the Chinese. Aside from a semihistorical account that an obscure Buddhist priest sailed to North America from China in the fifth century B.C., the first documented accounts of Chinese on this continent date back to the 1500s. Chinese servants were brought to Mexico aboard Spanish ships from the Philippines, and by the 1600s there was a substantial Chinese colony in Mexico

City. But Chinese immigrants began coming here in large numbers only after gold was discovered in California in 1848. At that time, thousands of prospectors descended on the state, and many peasant immigrants from China joined the Gold Rush. The Chinese called California *Gam Saan,* or Golden Mountain, and they hoped to take valuable pieces of it back home. Indeed, a few of the immigrants did stake claims to gold fields and managed to return to China with their wealth.

But the Chinese were largely laborers who eked out a living by working for white mine owners alongside white miners. At first, the Chinese got along fairly well, and aside from pranks played on them by the other miners, there were few serious incidents of prejudice. The mine owners, of course, appreciated their hard-working nature and willingness to accept lower wages. Eventually, however, the white mine workers became resentful of the competition, which they felt was ruining their own chances for better pay and working conditions. They argued that the Chinese were not planning to stay and were only taking what they could from America. None of them wanted to become Americans, the standard argument ran, and even if they did, they would never fit in. The miners coerced owners into firing the Chinese workers and pushed through all sorts of rules and regulations to exclude them. The Chinese miners were harassed, called heathens, and ridiculed for wearing pigtails. Some were beaten and some killed. *Gam Saan* had hardly lived up to its name.

But Chinese kept coming to America anyway. After the gold fever died, they were needed to build the transcontinental railroad from west to east; some 12,000 Chinese pitched in, playing a vital role in the massive construction project until its completion in 1869.

By the 1880s, there were more than 100,000 Chinese in America, most of them in California. They worked in wool, garment, and cigar factories. They competed with white workers in canneries, on farms, and in industrial plants. When they weren't living in company-owned shacks and sheds, they settled in Chinatowns, enclaves in the big cities where they could feel somewhat secure. But they were seldom secure.

Wherever the Chinese went, prejudice hounded them. In San

Francisco, a law was passed forbidding anyone to use a sidewalk while carrying a load on a pole, the traditional way Chinese carried their goods. "Not a Chinaman's chance" was a popular expression meaning that something was futile. More violence erupted, too. In Rock Springs, Wyoming, in 1885, miners massacred twenty-eight Chinese laborers because they would not join a union; elsewhere, Chinese were forcibly evicted from towns, sometimes tied to cattle and driven out by cowboys.

Congress responded to the hysteria — but in a negative way. The lawmakers had already refused citizenship to Chinese, and now it told would-be immigrants they had to stop coming in: it passed the Chinese Exclusion Act of 1882, which banned Chinese laborers or their wives from immigrating. Laws also barred Chinese from all sorts of occupations, including mining and manufacturing. "President Grover Cleveland supported the act," according to one recent account of the trials and tribulations of the Chinese,

> declaring the Chinese "an element ignorant of our Constitution and laws, impossible of assimilation with our people, and dangerous to our peace and welfare." Some states denied Chinese the right to testify against whites in courts. Many states prohibited them from owning property or from marrying whites. Twenty-five states required that Chinese children be taught in separate schools. After 1924, an American woman who married an "alien ineligible for citizenship" lost her own citizenship, and another law that took effect the same year barred the immigration of all Chinese women.[14]

Many Chinese gave up and returned home. The discriminatory laws had taken their toll: the Chinese population in America declined from about 100,000 in 1890 to some 60,000 by 1920.

Eventually there was a change for the better, but it took World War II to bring it about. With so many American men and women in the military during that period, there were more job opportunities for minority groups. The shipyards and other defense industries needed workers, and the Chinese were a valuable source. Several other factors helped get them back into the labor force. One was that the Japanese, with whom the U.S. was at war, had begun to add to anti-American sentiment in Asia by calling attention to the racist, exclusionary provisions of America's immigration laws. To deflect that criticism, the United States repealed the Chinese Exclusion Act in 1943, thereby allowing Chinese to come to the States. Another factor that worked in the Chinese people's favor was that China had resisted the Japanese and had been our ally during the war. This aroused a good deal of sympathy for the Chinese. Finally, Congress and the states later began passing various laws righting the wrongs that had hurt the Chinese. The ban on racially mixed marriages, for instance, was declared unconstitutional, and racial restrictions in housing were removed.

As more and more Chinese moved into mainstream industry, many of them also moved out of their Chinatowns and into other neighborhoods. Younger and more educated Chinese began arriving in America, and although it was sometimes more difficult for them to assimilate than, say, the Irish, they soon became Westernized, and citizens. Chinatowns remained the only safe havens for old-timers and for newly arrived and unskilled immigrants, but they were not what the new breed of Chinese-Americans wanted. The Chinatowns themselves also changed. Most of the immigrants from the 1950s to the 1980s, when the United States improved relations with the People's Republic of China, had come from Taiwan and Hong Kong. Nowadays, Chinatowns are home to Chinese from the mainland as well, and from all parts of Asia. So mixed has the Chinese population become in New York's Chinatown, to name but one, that the Cantonese, who were among the earliest settlers, complain that they are strangers in an all-Asian stew.[15]

New York's Chinatown is also different in another way. It is no longer just a place to live and run a few restaurants or a haven where Chinese get the financial and legal help they cannot always get in the outside world, but it is an enormously productive community as well. "They have turned Chinatown into the city's clothing-manufacturing center," says the report cited earlier.

> Its nearly six hundred factories have an annual payroll well over two hundred million dollars. It is also an impor-

> tant jewelry district now, with annual sales of a hundred million dollars in gold and diamonds. Its three hundred restaurants draw tourists and conventioneers.[16]

Impressive as that is, the Chinese in America have accomplished far more. While many Chinese-Americans still work in unskilled jobs, the prowess of Chinese scientists — many of whom are Nobel Prize winners — and the diligence of Chinese students have become legendary. The buildings of the noted architect I. M. Pei are familiar to most Americans. Chinese-Americans are lawmakers, judges, and television and newspaper journalists. It may seem naive to mention such things because they are, after all, exactly what many Americans have accomplished. It is important to remember, though, that the opportunity to achieve was certainly not available to the Chinese who came here during the Gold Rush days, and, indeed, it took decades for the Chinese to overcome the hostility that had robbed them of their civil rights. The muscle and bone of the Chinese should have made them the equals of whites when they were digging in the barren mountains for gold and throwing railroad track across the blazing hot desert. But that was not to be, for when it came to sharing the wealth of *Gam Saan,* Golden Mountain, the Chinese were considered unfit.

Although prejudice against the Chinese in America rarely erupts in violence today as it did in our early history, it remains in subtle forms. Interracial marriages are still largely frowned upon in America. Some people still think that Chinese — indeed all Asians — are "inscrutable," mysterious, different. There are even some in our society who believe that Chinese belong only in laundries, restaurants, garment factories, and in Charlie Chan movies. Others are angered when Chinese-American students win honors, when a Chinese "who wasn't even born here" makes more money than they do. Such attitudes can be eradicated only when we see how ridiculous it is to judge a person harshly because they might work harder than we do, because they worship a different god, or because of the shape of their eyes. Fortunately, it was the culture of the Chinese, the sum of all their special habits and customs, that allowed them to keep their self-esteem and gave them the confidence they needed to make it in America. It is too bad that the very culture that gave the Chinese so much strength was used as a basis for exclusion for so long. If Native Americans and African-Americans had been allowed to hang on to the cultures that were stripped from them, perhaps they would have fared far better than they have thus far.

The Japanese also came to America early, and by the late 1800s more than 15,000 had settled in Hawaii and California. Over the years, the number grew to 300,000, making the Japanese, at one time, the largest ethnic group in the United States.

Japanese immigrants worked on sugar plantations in Hawaii and were used as cheap labor in California's canneries and logging camps and on farms throughout the fertile Central Valley. Because they were ambitious and industrious and seemed to have a special feel for the land, they were soon quite successful in farming, and many bought their own gardens and farms.

But, as with the Chinese, the determination and hard work of the Japanese fueled resentment against them. Jealous farmers and landowners banded against the Japanese, calling attention to laws that stated that only free whites and people of African descent could become citizens. This meant that Japanese immigrants had to remain permanent aliens. Groups of "real" Americans, such as the Native Sons and Daughters of the Golden West — one of several anti-immigrant groups — teamed up with politicians, growers, and labor unions to hammer away at what they called the "yellow peril," the Japanese. In 1906, the San Francisco Board of Education brought racist attitudes into the classrooms by prohibiting Japanese children from attending public school. The next year, another law dictated that Japan was not to issue passports to laborers coming to the United States, and by 1924, Japanese immigration was severely restricted.

The situation worsened when the United States entered World War II some fifty years ago. While the war had some benefit for the Chinese-Americans, it devastated the Japanese living in America. Japan drew America into the war when it launched a sneak air attack on our naval base at Pearl Harbor, Hawaii, and killed many people. The attack was cowardly, and it is easy to understand why Americans were enraged at the Japanese and demanded revenge.

But America's retaliation against the Japanese went beyond the fierce land and sea battles that we fought to defeat the enemy. Immediately after the Pearl Harbor attack, curfews were imposed on Japanese neighborhoods in California and Hawaii, and the FBI arrested some 2,000 Japanese as "enemy aliens," even though there had been no acts of terrorism or sabotage. Not long afterward, the U.S. government took a drastic step that would later be widely regarded as one of the worst cases of injustice ever committed against people living in the States: it rounded up nearly 120,000 Japanese, some 70,000 of them American citizens, and shipped them to "camps" in the West. Forced from their homes, the Japanese had to live behind barbed wire and under armed guard in the desert regions of Tule Lake and Manzanar in California, and in remote areas of Arizona, Idaho, Utah, Arkansas, Colorado, and Wyoming.

The detainees ate in common mess halls, lived in barracks, and shared toilets and showers. They had to wear uniforms, and many had to do manual labor. Here's how one account described life in the camps:

> The most difficult problem proved to be the boredom and the monotony of camp life; it exacerbated tensions and magnified irritations, resulting in fights, riots, strikes and even homicides. Inmates complained constantly about the food, their neighbors, living conditions and camp administrators. Conflict between Issei and Nisei [first- and second-generation Japanese-Americans] added to the strain. Ideological arguments between those loyal to Japan and those who stood with the U.S. grew heated. The derogatory term *inu* [meaning dog in Japanese] was applied to those suspected of being spies or collaborators, and some of the *inu* were the victims of several beatings. Soldiers fired into striking crowds at Manzanar and Tule Lake. An Issei who wandered outside the gates and apparently did not understand when he was told to halt was shot dead by a soldier.[17]

Few of the prisoners could leave. One of the only ways out was for the men to join the military. Many refused — there was, after all, bitter irony in Japanese-Americans, with relatives behind barbed wire, fighting Nazi racists who were herding Jews into concentration camps and gas chambers. But many Japanese-Americans did enlist, hoping that by doing so they would prove their loyalty to the U.S. They did that — and more. In the history of the American armed forces, the exploits of the legendary 442nd Regimental Combat Team, made up of 33,000 Japanese-Americans, are unparalleled. Fighting for a country that had put them behind barbed wire, these Japanese-American soldiers went by the name Go For Broke; they suffered 9,000 casualties, including 600 killed, and became the most decorated unit in American military history. The group won an average of three medals for each man, and not only participated in some of the war's fiercest battles but sent its soldiers to liberate the German concentration camp at Dachau to free the Jews held there.

Pearl Harbor and the war against the Japanese undoubtedly played a large role in "relocating" the Japanese living in America. But one cannot ignore the fact that many American politicians, business owners, growers, and farm associations wanted the Japanese out of the way because so many of the Japanese were competing successfully in the huge agriculture industry.

After the war, the Japanese were freed and went back to their homes. A Civil Liberties Act was finally passed in 1988 in an effort to apologize. Each survivor of the camps was granted $20,000 in reparations.

Was the money enough to cover the painful experience? Can money alone make amends? Many Japanese would answer no to both questions. No amount of money can compensate them for the loss of their dignity and for the disruption of the tight family structure they were so proud of. Sadly, anti-Japanese sentiment is with us once again. Most of it is directed against Japanese competition from overseas. Japan is a mighty economic and industrial power whose products sometimes outshine ours. Japanese interests have bought up some of America's prize real estate, from Rockefeller Center in New York City to the Pebble Beach Golf Links in California, site of the 1992 U.S. Open tournament. Some 15,000 Japanese students and researchers show up at U.S. institutions every year, Japanese cars and electronic equipment are everywhere, and Japanese tourists spend more money than many

Americans will ever be able to. Once again, Americans are faced with having to cope with people who are "different" and who are doing very well here, if not better than they are. Let's hope that we have learned enough from past experience to prevent the seeds of jealousy and resentment from sprouting again into full-blown prejudice against an Asian group.

In many of our cities, other Asians — Koreans, Vietnamese, and Cambodians among them — have recently been assaulted and harassed by whites and blacks. In one case in New York City, a mob of black youths armed with baseball bats, knives, and bottles attacked three Vietnamese men, fracturing the skull of one of them while shouting anti-Korean slurs and yelling, "Koreans, what are you doing here?"[18] In that instance, the attackers couldn't tell the difference among Asian nationalities — and it didn't much matter, just as it didn't matter a few years earlier when a Chinese-American man in Detroit was beaten to death by two white auto workers who had made biased remarks about Asians and Japanese cars.

Such attacks against Asians should concern us not only because they hurt victims but because they hurt the entire nation. As New York City mayor David Dinkins put it after the attack on the Vietnamese men:

> This victim of hate and ignorance has a Vietnamese name. But this is not a case of violence against Vietnamese. This is violence against each of us. To those of you who participated in this mindless assault, I ask you: Where did you learn to hate people of a different skin color? Who taught you that people of a different ethnic origin than you have no right to live in peace and dignity in our city?[19]

The questions should be seriously considered, and when the teachers of racial and ethnic hatred are identified, they must be confronted and denounced.

HISPANICS

The word *Hispanic* refers to the people, language, and culture of Spain. Hispanics, thus, may be people with roots not only in Spain itself but in South or Central America, Mexico, or in the Caribbean islands such as Cuba, the Dominican Republic, and Puerto Rico.

Around 12 percent of our population, some 22 million people, is Hispanic. Mexicans form the largest group, accounting for about two-thirds of the Hispanics; 10 percent are Puerto Rican, and some 5 percent are Cuban. Hispanics are our second-fastest-growing minority group after the Asians.

Many Americans tend to forget — or perhaps aren't even aware — that when the Pilgrims stepped on Plymouth Rock, Spaniards had already visited our shores and established settlements. The Spanish explorer Juan Ponce de León, seeking the Fountain of Perpetual Youth, was the first European to explore Florida, in 1512; fifty years later, Pedro Menéndez de Aviles, a Spanish naval officer, founded St. Augustine, Florida, our oldest city; Santa Fe, in what is now New Mexico, was founded in 1606 by Spanish explorers. Later, missionary priests from Spain converted many Indians of California to Christianity and built some twenty missions along the length of California. Along with literature, language, and customs, the Spanish also introduced plants and animals to the New World — the horse, in fact, was introduced to the Americas by the Spanish, and it was the descendants of those first horses that Native Americans caught and rode. Spaniards also set up the first printing press in the Americas, in Mexico City. With such a rich history of involvement on both American continents, it hardly seems right that the contributions of the Spanish to our country are so often neglected, and overshadowed by those of the first English settlers.

Each of the groups of Hispanic people that has immigrated here has run into prejudice, and they do to this day. In fact, prejudice against Hispanics, especially Mexicans and Puerto Ricans, is often as strong as it is against blacks, a group with which the Hispanics are often linked, not only because some Hispanics are black or dark-skinned, but because both share the same economic and social problems. And once again, stereotypes feed the prejudice. The musical *West Side Story,* with its portrayals of switchblade-wielding Puerto Rican youths, has not helped to dispel the myths, nor has the current wave of television and movie "entertainment" that depicts Hispanics as drug dealers in gaudy gang jackets with names like Death's Angels on the backs or as grubby, ignorant "wetbacks" from Mexico swimming across the Rio Grande or climbing barbed wire fences in the dead of night to enter the U.S. illegally. Many Americans would typify a Puerto Rican in this way: an easily angered macho guy with a heavy gold chain around his neck who knifes a buddy while they're both high on crack during a fight over a Hispanic prostitute with AIDS who is wearing a dazzling red dress called Puerto Rican pink.

These lingering images of Hispanics as thugs and undesirables has made them the new media heavies. The Colombian cocaine cartel has replaced the Italian Mafia don, at least until a new ethnic group becomes the focus of attention and its problems are magnified all out of proportion and presented to the public as fact. If you or your friends have to use the words *typical* or *all* when referring to Hispanics, or to any other ethnic or racial group, watch out! You're buying into stereotyping. Yes, some Hispanics are lazy and noisy, and so are people of every other ethnic or racial group. Yes, some Hispanics are criminals, but as we have shown, crime is a result of environmental factors, not a trait imprinted on a person's genes. You should be able to take each of the negative comments about Hispanics for what they are: unfair and erroneous characterizations spread by bigots.

Being Hispanic in America very often means having to live in a separate world. According to the 1991 Census Bureau report, more than 20 percent of Hispanic families are poverty stricken, compared to around 9 percent of non-Hispanics (not including blacks, who have a 30 percent poverty rate). The median income of Hispanic American families is two-thirds that of non-Hispanics, and only about 10 percent of Hispanic men hold managerial or professional jobs, compared to some 27 percent of non-Hispanics.[20]

If Hispanics have a difficult time obtaining money on the job, they have an even tougher time when they try to borrow it from some banks. There is race bias in lending, no matter how many denials you hear from banks. One consumer advocacy group found recently that a major New York bank denied mortgage applications to whites only 17 percent of the time, while it denied 66 percent of the applications by American Indians, 44 percent by blacks, and 46 percent by Hispanics.[21] While more whites probably qualify because they have more money and less debt, the fact is that bank guidelines are sometimes too strict when applied across the board and do not take into account the relatively low wages of Hispanics and other groups who could well qualify if the banks would make some concessions.

Like blacks, Hispanics are also more likely than whites to serve jail time after being convicted of identical crimes. Even in prison, Hispanics draw harsher punishment than whites and are more often discriminated against when it comes to job assignments and living conditions. Because Hispanic prisoners are disciplined more often, this means that they have to spend more time behind bars waiting for parole. As a lawyer for inmates at a state prison in New York once observed, "If you have fifteen disciplinary infractions and ten of them are because of your race, you are going to stay in prison longer than a white person."[22]

Mexicans and Puerto Ricans seem to be the chief targets of anti-Hispanic prejudice and discrimination. The Cubans have had their share of problems, but they are the smallest Hispanic group here, and they have had, in the opinion of sociologists and authorities on race relations, several things in their favor: blacks and other dark-skinned people were not all that prevalent in the Cubans who moved to the mainland after Fidel Castro took over Cuba, they are economically self-sufficient and have gained political clout, and they are vigorously anti-Communist, which has set well with Americans who do not appreciate Fidel Castro.

Mexico's relationship to the United States is another matter and has a long history. It all started in 1835 when Texas, then Mexican territory, declared its independence and, ten years later, was annexed to the U.S. Then came the U.S.-Mexican War. When it was over, the U.S. had acquired half the land that once belonged to Mexico, including all or parts of Arizona, California, Colorado, Nevada, New Mexico, Texas, Utah, and Wyoming.

With the land, the United States of course got Mexicans, a lot of them. The California Gold Rush brought in more, and others came later, lured by the prospect of making a better living here. Sometimes the Mexicans were invited, as they were during World War II by a treaty that allowed an unlimited number of temporary workers, called *braceros,* to fill agricultural jobs here. By the end of the program in 1964, more than 4.5 million Mexicans had come to work temporarily in the United States, far exceeding the number of permanent legal immigrants. That phenomenon created the lasting impression that Mexican immigrants go back and forth across the border, with their ultimate destination Mexico and not the U.S.[23]

Legal immigration, which had also increased steadily over the years, was eventually checked. But illegal immigrants, without having to cross an ocean to get here as did immigrants from Europe and Asia, started pouring in at the rate of hundreds of thousands a year. By the early 1980s, some 55 percent of all undocumented immigrants in the U.S. came from Mexico, accounting for an estimated two-thirds of all Mexican immigration.[24]

The U.S. government has cracked down over the years. It has erected barbed wire fences and high metal walls along the long, often floodlit border, conducted surprise raids on businesses that employ illegal workers, and deported millions. But still they come, sometimes risking their lives to cross the guarded borders. And when they do, most manage to keep their ties to their families in Mexico, something that few other immigrant groups can do.

This clannishness, along with the general perception of the Mexican workers' nomadic existence, has created great friction between them and non-Hispanics. Many Americans also believe that Mexican immigrants are not learning English and adjusting to our culture as quickly as other immigrants, are straining the welfare system, will have no positive effect on our government, and don't pay their fair share of taxes.

While some of that may be true, the fact is that many Mexicans — native sons and daughters as well as their descendants — have been a credit to their ethnic group. For instance, Dr. Celestino Fernandez, who came to the U.S. as a boy, became one of the youngest college administrators in the U.S. when he was promoted to associate vice president of the University of Arizona at the age of thirty-seven; in 1974, two Chicanos were elected to U.S. governorships: Jerry Apodaca in New Mexico and Raul Castro in Arizona; and then there is, of course, Cesar Chavez, leader of the United Farm Workers, who helped Chicanos in their struggle for better working conditions.

Many scholars have tried to dispel some of the negative perceptions some non-Hispanic Americans have about Mexicans. Recently, George Vernez and David Ronfeldt of the RAND Corporation's Program for Research on Immigration Policy concluded that Mexican immigration has changed and that growing numbers come here to stay, not just to work awhile and return home. They also point out that the newly legalized immigrants, both naturalized Mexicans and native Mexican-Americans, "will exert an increasing political influence on local and national affairs." Moreover, they add, the Mexican-American community will probably become increasingly involved in forming U.S. policy toward not only Mexico but also Central and South America.[25]

It is true that a growing number of Mexicans — and any other foreign group — without language or occupational skills puts great stress on our educational and economic systems and increases the demand for public services. But America's strength is in its racial and ethnic mix, no matter what the doomsayers in our midst say. If more agencies, public and private, took an interest in educating immigrants and in retraining them for jobs, not only would some of the prejudice die, but the country's economy would benefit. In the case of the Mexicans, they are not only our close neighbors, but they have already given as much as they have received from our country. Considering the land they used to own, some would say much more.

While many Mexican immigrants have to sneak into the United States, the other large Hispanic group, the Puerto Ricans, have had free and easy access to our shores because Puerto Rico has been under U.S. control since 1898, and its residents have been U.S. citizens since 1917. Puerto Rico is a commonwealth nation, which means it elects its own governor and is voluntarily united with the United States. Puerto Ricans don't have to pay federal taxes, and they cannot vote in U.S. elections. (They can, however, be drafted to serve in the U.S. armed forces.)

But even though they are U.S. citizens, even though they can travel freely to this country and live and work here without having to deal with all the red tape that other immigrants must, the life of a Puerto Rican in our major eastern cities — the largest population is in New York City — is still that of an immigrant, and it is not always a happy one. Their poverty rate is among the highest, if not the highest, in many areas. Large numbers of Puerto Ricans are unskilled and uneducated, and live in some of the worst sections of our cities. There is a high proportion of drug addiction and AIDS among Puerto Ricans, and a high proportion of young Puerto Rican women are unwed mothers. To make matters worse, their relationship to other Hispanic groups, to blacks, with whom they have had to compete for work, and to other ethnic groups, is quite often tense, to say the least. While Puerto Ricans generally make a public show of solidarity with blacks and other Latinos, there is often mutual distrust beneath it all. In a sense, it is the same atmosphere in which the Irish and the Italians coexisted when the Irish were the dominant force. It seems frivolous to say, "Well, that's the American way," but so it goes. The ones who have staked their claims to a block almost always torment the newcomers if they are not members of the ethnic or racial club.

Here's how one man of Puerto Rican descent, born in Harlem, a predominantly black neighborhood in New York City, described his experiences in New York:

> When as a group of Puerto Rican kids, we decided to go swimming to Jefferson Park Pool, we knew we risked a fight and a beating from the Italians. And when we went to La Milagrosa Church in Harlem, we knew we risked a fight and a beating from the blacks. But when we went over to Cooney's Hill, we risked dirty looks, disapproving looks, and questions from the police, like, "What are you doing in this neighborhood?" and "Why don't you kids go back where you belong?" Where we belonged! Man, I had written compositions about America. Didn't I belong on the Central Park tennis courts, even if I didn't know how to play? Couldn't I watch Dick play? Weren't these policemen working for me, too?"[26]

The next time you encounter a person who doesn't speak English too well, think a little about your parents or grandparents if they came here from a non-English-speaking foreign country. Try to imagine how they must have felt when someone made fun of their accents or their inability to use English well. How do you think they felt when a clerk was impatient with them, when people made comments to them like, "For God's sake, why don't you learn the language?" or when they were subjected to ethnic or racial insults? The advice about remembering your immigrant forebears every so often is directed mainly at so-called Americanized young people, those a couple of generations or more removed from their immigrant roots, whose lifestyles are thoroughly American. They are the ones who most often get a bit too judgmental and who sometimes think that they're a lot better than "foreigners." The advice also applies to recent immigrants, many of whom are so clannish that they exclude everyone not of their ethnic background, and they, too, can be bigoted. If you are a recent immigrant, it is understandable that you prefer to be with people who have the same background as you and that you perhaps even mistrust others. But sooner or later, you must become part of the stream, not giving up your culture, but adding the mainstream culture to your own.

For everyone, Americanized or not, it is all a matter of putting ourselves in someone else's skin. Try to imagine what Japanese-Americans must have felt when they were kept behind barbed wire in a country where they had worked for so long or where they were born. Think of those Japanese-Americans who fought against the Germans for the U.S. during World War II. How do you think a Chinese laborer felt when he was given laundry to do because it was woman's work or when he had to endure being called "He-She" by his tormenters? Or an Italian who had to sit in the back of the church, an Irishman who "need not apply," a Hispanic who had to endure being called spic, which comes from "No spica English"?

We haven't said much about the German immigrants, but they, too, suffered from our bigots. Millions came here in the 1800s, and during World War I, the German-influenced names of several common things were changed because we were fighting Germany. Frankfurters, for Frankfurt, in Germany, became hot dogs; hamburgers, for the city of Hamburg, became Salisbury steaks. During World War II, many German-Americans were accused of being pro-Hitler, and their language was banned from some schools. Fortunately for them, General Dwight Eisenhower, who led our troops in Europe during the war and who later became president of the United States, was of German descent.

Without the German influence in America, we probably wouldn't be singing "Silent Night," a German hymn, or waiting up for Santa Claus.

And what of the Norwegians? True, they came in smaller numbers than the others we've talked about, and their lot here was better than that of the Irish, the Italians, the Jews, and the Hispanics. They probably explored the New World in 1000 A.D., a lot earlier than Columbus and all the other European explorers, and they were in America long before the Civil War. They were pioneers, farmers, and woodsmen, and they helped build America.

"When the valley of the Red River of the North was settled," wrote one American of Norwegian descent,

> it had the greatest concentration of Norwegians outside of Norway. Its great bonanza farms began to harvest millions of bushels of wheat annually and it became known as the Breadbasket of the World. The wonder is not that so many of these first settlers succumbed, but that so many survived. A partial catalogue of the trials that beset them would show such entries as grasshopper plagues, blizzards, long Arctic winters, stupefying hot shadeless summers, prairie fires, earthquakes, cyclones, tornadoes, electrical storms, the devastation of blackbirds and gophers and the chinch bug, hail storms, torrential rains that turned the grain to rot, poor seed and ignorance of good farming practices, oxen running wild, horses and cattle driven insane by mosquitoes, nerve-shattering winds, droughts, crop failures, money panic . . . lost or stolen livestock, stem rust in the spring wheat, the constant threat of attack by Indians, killing strikes by pneumonia and typhoid fever, death by freezing, backbreaking labor without end, and the aching loneliness. And yet Americans used to call them Norwegian Indians and blockheads.[27]

The next time you're tempted to crack an ethnic joke or make a racial slur, think about what you have read in this chapter about your own immigrant ancestors, who were tough enough to stick it out in an often hostile place.

7 • SEXISM
Oppressing the Majority

Of all the plagues with which the world is curst, of every ill, a woman is the worst.
— George Granville, Baron Lansdowne, *The British Enchanters*

I realize that unless women organize, support each other, and force change, nothing basic is going to happen. Not even with the best of men.
— Gloria Steinem, 1969

Throughout history, women have been both worshiped and abused by men. Men love them madly, marry them, care for them, and have children with them. Men give up thrones and professions for women, start wars over them, write songs about them, get into fights because of them, and make fools out of themselves over them. Men thank their mothers profusely for the "million things she gave me" and dote on "Daddy's little girl," who is "sugar and spice and everything nice."

But the things that men do *for* women are often overshadowed by the things they do *to* them. The abuse ranges from ignoring women's opinions to forcible rape and the killing of infant daughters, ultimate expressions of men's power and control over what many men consider the "weaker sex." Women have been denied the right to vote, deprived of education, sexually harassed, limited to certain kinds of work, and, when lucky enough to land the same job as a man, have often been paid less than he. "Keep 'em barefoot and pregnant" was the attitude of a generation of young not so long ago. In his poem "The Vampire," Rudyard Kipling wrote:

A fool there was and he made his prayer
(Even as you and I!)
To a rag and a bone and a hank of hair
(We called her the woman who did not care)
But the fool he called her his lady fair —
(Even as you and I!).

And in another of his outrageous statements about females, Kipling purported to put women in their place with "A woman is only a woman, but a good cigar is a smoke." It should be obvious that, more often than not, the world has truly been a man's down through the ages.

The prejudice that men have shown toward women is as serious, and as reprehensible, as all of the other prejudices we have been discussing. Why should a woman be discriminated against, or abused, because of her sex? Are the reasons behind this phenomenon the same as the ones that apply in the case of, say, Jews and blacks? That is to say, are men threatened by women? Do they need a scapegoat when things aren't going well? Do men really believe that women are inferior to men, as the Nazis believed the Jews were inferior or white supremacists believe that blacks are?

Some men are convinced that women are actually intellectually inferior or that they are too emotional to be managers. A few even try to justify that notion with science, arguing that perhaps women's brains are "wired" differently or that female hormones somehow interfere with a woman's reasoning process. A suggestion one hears from time to time is that women are better at verbal tasks than men but worse at mathematical ones. Because of that stereotype, many math teachers tend to ignore female students in favor of males. As a result, many young women do not develop confidence in their math ability — and they do have that ability, just as men do — and quite often score lower than men in math tests.

Most men who regard women as beneath them are not usually referring to a woman's intellectual capacity. Both heredity and environment play key roles in the development of intelligence, in men *and* women, and no one knows how much of each factor goes into the formula, so it would be impossible to prove that one sex has it all over the other. Chances are that any man who believes that all men are smarter is not exceptionally brainy himself. If he were, he wouldn't be making such a foolish statement. Again, ignorance plays a starring role in prejudice.

Men who say women are inferior usually mean that women are physically weaker and that because of the physical difference, women must be protected by, sometimes subject to, men. It is an ages-old concept, one that has been handed down from generation to generation of men, sometimes through word and deed, sometimes by tradition and culture, other times through more modern means of education, such as advertisements that show women doing only "women's work" and assign them roles and behavior that put women in a subservient position.

It is perhaps understandable, given women's roles over the years, why men so often feel the way they do toward women. Here's one explanation, offered nearly sixty years ago, of how those roles were formed:

> The pursuit of war and the chase gave the male the advantage of superior bodily strength and initiative. The protector of the family became the founder of the state and the warrior became the ruler. With the decrease of warfare and the rise of the institution of property, men more and more turned their attention to the industrial arts. The talent for invention forced out by militarism was used for the more specialized development of the arts, which women had founded. Men discovered that labor was the best means for satisfying their multiplying wants, and a partial realignment of the social services took place.
>
> By preference, men appropriated the work requiring skill and strength, while women more and more withdrew from agriculture and the other outdoor callings to devote themselves to the arts and crafts which centered in the immediate household life. With the rise of feudalism in Europe the woman of leisure, the "lady," appeared. The wife or daughter of the feudal chief, of the "gentleman," must abstain from gainful or menial toil. Thus war devel-

> oped the false ideal of chivalry of helpless dependence of the female on the male.[1]

In many societies throughout the world, women still perform traditional roles. They do the weaving and sewing, the washing and the cooking. Their place is in the home, as mothers, servants, wives. Quite often, they have very few rights, and when the men are talking, they are seen but rarely heard. Some clergymen of limited understanding would even lead us to believe that this harsh treatment of women is punishment for the role that, according to the Bible, Eve played a long, long time ago, tempting Adam, bringing evil into the world, and getting her and Adam banished from the idyllic Garden of Eden. After all, according to the Bible, Jehovah did say to Eve,

> I will greatly multiply thy sorrow and thy conception; in sorrow thou shalt bring forth children; and thy desire shall be to thy husband [meaning she shall be subject to her husband], and he shall rule over thee.

Tertullian, a famous Christian who was born a hundred years or so after Christ, wrote:

> God's sentence still hangs over your sex and His punishment weights down upon you. You are the devil's gateway; you are she who first violated the forbidden tree and broke the law of God. It was you coaxed your way around him whom the devil had not the force to attack. With what ease you shattered that image of God: man! Because of the death you merited, the Son of God had to die.[2]

And men never let women forget that. At one time in many countries a woman was not allowed to eat the food she had grown or the flesh of the animals she had killed until her husband had filled himself, and then she could eat only what he left on the table. Women were forbidden to discipline male children; they could be put to death by their husbands or could be left for another woman and sent to prison whenever the husband decided it was time for a change. The familiar image of the caveman dragging a woman off to his cave is no artist's fiction: among Australian tribes, when a man wanted a wife, all he had to do was creep up behind her, hit her on the head with a club, toss her over his shoulder, and take her away. If she survived, she became a wife; if not, the man was blameless because he had only done what was expected, and he would only try again.

When these and similar views of how women are to be treated are continually reinforced by the ignorant, they only strengthen the notion of woman's servile role; they can also do enormous damage to some women's self-esteem if taken seriously. The claim that women have to pay the price for what the First Woman may have done to Adam is no different from the accusation that because the Jews murdered Christ all Jews must be punished. Any woman who accepts the crazy notion that women bear the guilt of Eve is as misguided and as in need of counseling as any Jew today who accepts the charge that he or she was indirectly responsible for the death of Christ and therefore deserves all of the prejudice leveled against Jews.

There is no historical record other than the Bible to document the existence of Adam and Eve, let alone Eve's role as the first bewitcher. But the women who were persecuted as witches in Europe and America in the sixteenth and seventeenth centuries are very much part of the historical record, and their plight bears mentioning here because these were women who endured the worst kind of man's irrational hostility toward the opposite sex.

The men who persecuted women suspected of being witches were often members of the clergy — including officials of the Inquisition that persecuted other heretics — who took to heart the ominous words of the Bible's Book of Exodus: "Thou shalt not suffer a witch to live." Women accused of being witches supposedly communicated with the devil or had sexual intercourse with him, worked all kinds of spells upon humans, or caused plagues and natural disasters. While the hierarchy of the Christian church in the Middle Ages strongly opposed the persecution of supposed witches, an ignorant and superstitious population, often fired up by equally ignorant clerics, made life truly hellish for the unfortunate women who were singled out for punishment. A woman might be accused of being a witch simply because she behaved strangely, perhaps because of some emotional illness, or because she refused to go to church or even because she had property or money that a jealous neighbor or a cruel judge wanted confiscated. It was no different from what happened over the centuries to the Jews, whose land and money were taken by envious, threatened anti-Semites who also accused Jews of being heretics and of the ritual killing of Christian babies.

Suspected witches were tortured to get them to confess that they flew around on brooms, held Black Masses to worship Satan, or ate the bodies of sacrificed children. When found guilty, they were burned at the stake, boiled in oil, or crushed to death. No one knows how many women were executed as witches, but the estimates range into the millions.

One notorious witch prosecutor in England, where many witches were tried and executed in the 1500s and 1600s, was Matthew Hopkins, a vile man known as the Witchfinder-General. Accompanied by a band of misfits and troublemakers, Hopkins prowled the countryside hunting for poor, deformed, and disturbed women who fit the popular image of witches. When he found a likely candidate, he tied her up, collected a large fee from the county or private parties for discovering a witch, and brought her to "trial." In 1645, in one county alone, Hopkins hanged sixty women, pocketing about twenty shillings a head.

While nowhere near as many suspected witches were executed in America as in Europe, trials for people accused of practicing witchcraft were held in Colonial times, and a number of women (along with a fewer number of men) were hanged. Salem, Massachusetts, became infamous for the witchcraft trials that were held there in 1692. Among the clergymen responsible for much of the hysteria and panic that brought on the trials was Cotton Mather, a vociferous "hellfire" minister in Boston. Mather was obsessed with witches, and he wrote a good deal about them. One person he wrote about was a thirteen-year-old girl, Martha Goodwin, who had been invited to live in Mather's home. The girl, according to Mather, threw fits, became rigid, spoke in strange languages, tried to fly, and rode an invisible horse. Mather noted it all down, including one of her statements as she fought off demons:

"How many Fits more am I to have?" the girl was quoted as saying.

> Pray can ye tell me how long it shall be how long it shall be before you are hang'd for what you have done? You are filthy witches to my knowledge. You would have killed me but you cannot. I do not fear you. You would have thrown Mr. Mather down stairs but you could not.[3]

Stories like this were just what superstitious citizens needed to hear. Writers have pointed out that Mary Goodwin was probably either a talented actress or that she suffered from an emotional disorder or had epileptic seizures. But such explanations were not offered in those days, and the hysteria spread. Soon the celebrated Salem trials, spurred by Mather's inflammatory writings, were underway. They started after a West Indies woman who had been brought to Salem by another minister, Samuel Parris, began telling scary stories about voodoo rites to a group of young women who claimed later that they had been bewitched. One said she was bitten on the wrist by an invisible witch, and she showed off the teeth marks. Another said she had fits; the others claimed they were pinched and strangled by demons. On the basis of such flimsy testimony, an elderly woman was tried on witchcraft charges, convicted, and hanged. Panic spread when several adults in the community started throwing fits and observing strange events.

Soon, witches were everywhere. Anyone who seemed a bit odd was suspect. More than 150 people, most of them women, were sent to prison; eleven were hanged, and one was pressed to death. Among those who went to the gallows was Goody Martin, and the story they tell about her shows how ignorant the community was in those days. When Goody Martin was waiting for the noose to be placed around her neck, it was said, she chanted words that made the rope spring out of the hangman's hands so that he couldn't tie the knot. Finally a crow flew by and cawed out to the hangman that he should use a noose made of a willow branch. The hangman took the advice, and Goody Martin was executed.[4]

Fortunately, the ministers and the townspeople came to their senses before more women were put to death. Cotton Mather's minister-father, Increase Mather, agreed that innocent people had died. A judge, Samuel Sewell, publicly regretted his role in sentencing the women. The governor, William Phips, finally put a stop to the trials, but only after his wife had been accused of sympathizing with an accused witch.[5] And the twelve jurors who had sentenced so many innocent women to death issued the following statement:

> We justly fear that we were sadly deluded and mistaken for which we are much disquieted and distressed in our minds, and do therefore humbly beg forgiveness first of God for Christ's sake for this our Error. . . . We do heartily ask forgiveness of you all whom we have justly offended, and do declare according to our present minds we would none of us do such things again on such grounds for the whole World.[6]

Happily, women no longer have to suffer the ravings of a Cotton Mather — although on occasion we do hear the word *witch* used as an insult to mean an ugly elderly woman or a woman who is difficult to get along with. (*Witch* can also mean an alluring, provocative woman, but that's not what a young man generally means when he snarls it out at a female. The wicked witch in the *Wizard of Oz,* unfortunately, is what he sees, not her good sister-witch, Glinda.)

Witch trials have vanished, but the abuse of women in other ways has not. The maltreatment that we hear about today takes two forms. The first involves actual physical or emotional abuse — crimes such as rape, wife-beating, and sexual harassment. The second is the so-called double standard, which simply means applying more severe principles — moral, legal, and cultural — to women than to men. Make no mistake about it. Both spring from prejudice against women and from men's need to control them, and as such, they are just as poisonous as all the other prejudices that beset our society.

VIOLENCE AGAINST WOMEN

Two kinds of outright violence are often directed against women: forcible rape and physical assault, often by a husband or boyfriend. Both are expressions of aggression by men who need to show that they hold power over women. But so, too, is sexual harassment, which is when a person physically accosts another person (usually a man to a woman) — by fondling, touching, or making some other direct contact — without that person's consent or when someone makes a another person feel uncomfortable or threatened by making unwelcome sexual remarks in his or her presence.

Let's look first at forcible rape, in which a man attacks a woman and forces her to have sex with him. (There is another kind of rape, statutory rape, which is when a man has sexual relations with a woman under the legal age of consent, usually eighteen, whether or not she agrees. But we'll use the word *rape* here to mean the forcible kind.)

Reports of forcible rape have increased significantly throughout the world. Almost every day we read of cases of incest, which is sexual intercourse, often forced, between related individuals; of young women raped at parties by male high school and college students; and of women raped by soldiers after a battle. Because rape is a prime example of how women are mistreated, and because so many of the assaults are committed by young men, it is vital that our young male readers know more about the sort of people who commit the crime and why.

What many people believe about rape is not true; that is, it is not just a case of an aggressive man forcing a woman to have sex with him because he wants sex. It is a violent crime, like beating someone up or killing them, and it is usually committed by an emotionally disturbed person who needs to express hostility and terrify the victim. Most men who rape have criminal records for other forms of aggression, and they most certainly need help, just as the women upon whom they prey need help, both medical and psychological counseling, after an assault.

To add insult to injury, when a rape case goes to trial, the victim is often portrayed as having provoked the assault. She has worn sexy clothing, goes the standard argument, or she invited the attack by going to someone's home after a night of drinking in a bar. Jurors have, in fact, refused to convict accused rapists because they simply did not believe the woman's story that she was the innocent victim. Granted that when there are no witnesses to the crime and when it is the woman's word against the rapist's — lawyers call such a situation a "He said; she said" case — it is often difficult to prove that an assault has taken place. This may be especially true when the rape case involves two people who were together, perhaps partying, before the alleged attack. Two recent and widely publicized cases fall into that category. One involved William Kennedy Smith, nephew of Senator Edward M. Kennedy of Massachusetts. Smith was accused of raping a young woman who had gone willingly with him to the family's home from a local bar. He was acquitted. The other involved former heavyweight boxing champion Mike Tyson, accused of raping a woman who had gone to his hotel room. Tyson was found guilty and sent to prison. Jurors have a difficult job in such cases, and they tend to be suspicious when they learn that the woman agreed to be with the alleged rapist before the suspected attack. The jurors do not really know what led up to the attack or whether the woman was willing or whether the woman made the whole thing up to get back at the man for something else. And when there is doubt, a juror cannot and should not convict.

The trouble is, verdicts that go against women in rape cases prevent many other women from reporting rapes. Women who have been through the terror of a rape, and have read about how other rape victims were forced to relive the awful experience and then were accused of improper behavior just don't want to endure a trial.

Authorities on rape say that a lot of people believe that women are responsible for how men behave sexually and that "good women don't get raped, and bad women deserve it." Said one authority recently after three Long Island, New York students were acquitted of sexually assaulting another student after getting her drunk, "We have 10,000 years of prejudice to overcome, and women have no credibility."[7]

Sometimes, too, a jury's verdict can be based on race. When a black woman was assaulted by a white man in the South years ago, an all-white jury often rejected the woman's argument and acquitted the white man; black men charged with raping white women were, on the other hand, usually found guilty. Such miscarriages of justice may not happen as often today, but there have been recent cases in which race may have biased jurors. In all fairness, though, most juries do their difficult jobs very well, and the charges of race bias that are sometimes raised when a verdict does not go the way a minority group wishes are often based more on anger than on the truth.

It is difficult, however, for any black woman to understand a jury that has exonerated a white man accused of raping her, just as it is difficult for many women not to side automatically with any woman who claims she was raped. Men, on the other hand, often make equally quick decisions; some become defensive and tend to blame the woman's "come-on" for any assault that may have occurred. Unfortunately, some women also believe that women sometimes put themselves in positions to be taken advantage of.

The next time you hear about a rape case, try to put your own biases aside and look behind the gossip and the headlines. Remember that in our system of justice, a person is innocent until proven guilty. When a person is accused, he or she must get the benefit of the doubt. As logical as that general rule might seem, it is not always easy to apply. In an instance of rape, this rule must obviously apply to the accused, the defendant. Unfortunately, though, the victim in rape cases is also sometimes under suspicion, and the victim becomes the defendant as lawyers try to tear her story apart.

Again, you must ask some difficult questions. If you have made a snap judgment, do you know why? Did the color of the victim and the alleged assailant influence your decision? Do you think your own sex had anything to do with it? Do you believe that women attract rapists by dressing and acting sexy? If the alleged rape victim had been out drinking with the man accused of assaulting her, should that discount her story of rape? If the woman goes willingly to the man's home, does that mean he is blameless if he forces himself on her? Is any woman who dresses and acts provocatively fair game? And even if she does appear to be "just asking for it," does that justify being brutally attacked? What is the difference between a seduction and a rape? If you are a young man, do you think you are different from a rapist you have read about? If so, in what way?

There are many more questions to ask yourself, but two are most important: Do you believe that a woman must be submissive to a man? And, if so, is violence that reinforces that view to be condoned? Anyone who can honestly answer yes to those questions is not only dead wrong but prejudiced against women and a bully as well. Prejudice of all kinds is driven by wrong-headed impressions about a person. Unfortunately, those impressions all too often lead to violent behavior aimed at showing someone just who is boss.

In the case of rape, you must, as in examining any act of prejudice, try to put yourself in the victim's position. Women can do that easily, because they can imagine someone raping them and how they'd feel if it happened. Men must look at it a bit differently. If you are a young man, how would you like to be violently forced to do something against your will, perhaps even be sexually abused by another man, as happens often? How would you feel if your mother, sister, or girlfriend were the victim of a rape? It is imperative that you identify with women who are maltreated, that you understand what they have been through, that you sympathize with them. From childhood, men have been led to believe — and often the learning comes not from deliberate instruction but from subtle signals all around them — that they are better than women, that women are their possessions. These stereotypes must be dismissed, and men have as much responsibility in wiping them out as do women.

Rape is one example of how some men mistreat women. Wife beating is another. It is estimated that two million women are beaten by their husbands every year, and no one knows how many unmarried women are battered by their so-called lovers. Such abuse goes on just about everywhere. In some cultures, it is even condoned: wives may be beaten and even killed if they have dishonored their families, and nothing is done to punish the assailants.

Tough laws dictating what women may and may not do are especially evident in Muslim countries. While the Koran, Islam's holy book of revelations, says that women must behave toward their husbands "in like manner as their husbands should behave toward them," it also notes: "But the men ought to have a superiority over them." Islamic fundamentalists tolerate no "loose" behavior by their women, who may be whipped if they refuse to wear their veils or if they smoke. Iran, a nation ruled by Islamic fundamentalists, is one place where women are treated harshly if they dare to demonstrate for civil rights: torture, imprisonment, and sometimes death are the penalties for refusing to submit to the will of men.

Women in India, too, have had to suffer. Marriages there are often arranged, and when the bride (who is valued not for love but for the dowry she brings with her) begins housekeeping in the home of her husband's family, she is usually treated as a servant and quite often abused by the relatives. Some women's groups have charged that when marriages do not work out in India, the family sometimes gets rid of the bride. It's called bride burning because some of the women have been set on fire. Other harassed women commit suicide.[8]

Such deeply rooted cultural biases against women may not be prevalent in America, but physical abuse is common. Sometimes, the men who abuse their wives have been, themselves, abused as children; or they are sociopathic individuals who are prone to all manner of antisocial behavior, from breaking windows to battering people. Other times, the frustrations and problems of life — loss of a job, poverty, or a bad marriage — become too much for some men, and they take their bitterness out on their wives. Whatever the underlying reason, the man who beats his wife is quite often a controlling person who turns violent when he feels he is no longer in control.

As in the case of rape, many abused women do not report the assault because they are too embarrassed to discuss it or because they fear that their husband will punish them by beating them again. Some even blame themselves for the assault and believe they deserve the ill-treatment. But other women do not suffer in silence, and they respond to violence with violence, sometimes killing husbands who abused them. In several of these cases, the women have been granted clemency, and their sentences have been commuted.

Wife beating, like rape, is a crime against women that cannot be justified, no matter how pressured the man feels. And as in the case of rape, preventing such abuse requires that young men change the way they feel about women. Women are not mere sexual receptacles, nor maidservants, nor nonthinking objects.

Young men have to learn to express themselves, to communicate, without using their fists. Resorting to violence to make a point is not the best answer. It may sometimes be justified, in war or in self-defense, but not when it is used to express one's negative feelings about someone's sex, color, religion, or ethnic background.

The perception of women as sexual objects leads us to the third kind of abuse women must endure: sexual harassment. Whether it involves actual physical contact or not, sexual harassment is still an assault, an intrusion, and an insult. In the worst cases, women are refused jobs, promotions, or, in school, grades, unless they have sex with the man who controls their work or studies. In the workplace, sexual harassment can mean "Put out or get out." In school, it's known as "An A for a lay."

Perhaps the most compelling example of sexual harassment came during the 1991 U.S. Senate confirmation hearings involving Judge Clarence Thomas, President Bush's choice for a seat on the U.S. Supreme Court, and Anita Hill, a law professor at the University of Oklahoma. Hill charged that nearly ten years before, while she was working as a lawyer in an office then run by Thomas, he made several unwelcome obscene remarks to her and pestered her for dates. She said she was offended by the comments and refused to go out with him. When Hill's charges were made public, under oath, during Thomas's confirmation hearings, he vehemently denied each and every one of them, also under oath.

Obviously, one of the two people had to be lying. But which one was it? The debate over the case was a fierce one, and one that revolved around issues of politics, feminism, and race, because both people involved were black and the senators who were judging them were white.

When Hill told her side of the story, many people did not believe her, arguing that she had accused Thomas because he had spurned her own advances, or that she had made the whole thing up, either as part of an effort to "get" Thomas and stop him from taking a seat on the high court, or because she was prone to fantasies. Many women sided against her, and both men and women questioned why she had not brought out her charges years ago and why she continued over the years to telephone Thomas and see him on occasion — hardly, said her antagonists, behavior one would expect from a woman who had been subjected to the vile treatment she had supposedly received.

Thomas, too, was disbelieved by many. Some feminists immediately proclaimed him guilty, senators who had opposed his nomination from the beginning considered it another reason to keep him off the court, and other witnesses before the investigating committee tried to establish that he had been guilty of sexual harassment on other occasions.

Unfortunately, most of the defenders and critics of the two principals had some personal or political motive other than just trying to get at the truth, and in that regard the hearings were a tragedy. The hearings were not supposed to be a trial in the usual sense — had they been, most of the testimony would have been unacceptable in court — but they turned into a trial nevertheless, one without any of the usual rules of conduct that protect both the accused and the accuser. Witnesses gave testimony over the telephone without being sworn in; they offered psychological motives without having any expertise whatsoever in psychology; they offered hearsay evidence; they made accusations without proof; they gave knee-jerk, stereotyped opinions without considering both sides of the issue.

When the hearings were over, Thomas was confirmed by a Senate vote of fifty-two to forty-eight, one of the narrowest margins ever in an appointment of an associate justice of the Supreme Court.

The truth behind this accusation may never be known, and the fact that one of the two was lying is troubling, especially considering that both people were telling their stories under oath and are lawyers whose duty is to uphold the law. If anything good came out of the hearings, it was not that right or the truth prevailed — the vote to confirm did not establish guilt or innocence — but that they focused attention on the widespread problem of sexual harassment, on why so many women do not report instances of it, and on how a woman who does make an accusation of sexual harassment often comes out looking like the villain.

Sexual harassment must be taken more seriously than it has

been, for it is another form of rape. During the hearings, women were urged to stop being afraid to come forward (although the way the hearings were conducted did not inspire confidence), to take good notes in the workplace whenever someone says or does something offensive, and to tell a friend when an incident occurs. But sexual harassment is not merely a women's issue. Men of all ages have to understand that it is simply not true that "boys will be boys," that women are there to be fondled, subjected to dirty jokes and obscene overtures, and otherwise threatened and held hostage by sex bullies. Men must also be made aware that every time a woman acts friendly, even flirtatiously, toward them it is not an invitation to have sex. Unfortunately, innocent behavior is too often taken as a come-on, and a man is apt to read more into it than intended.

On the other hand, there is also a danger in misinterpreting innocent behavior as sexual harassment. A woman has to be able to read correctly the signals that come from a man, just as he must. He might, after all, merely be acting in a way that is generally acceptable, but in the mind of an overly conservative individual could be misread as promiscuous. Men and women, after all, have to interact sexually and socially — romance and meaningful relationships are essential human endeavors — and if every touch, every remark, every action, is seen as sexual harassment, then men and women will avoid one another out of fear. Every pat on the back should not be replaced with a handshake. Such an overreaction will not foster a healthy relationship between men and women.

If you're a young man, you must know a women well before you touch her or tell her an off-color joke, so that you are sure she will not be offended by your behavior. Ask yourself whether sexual innuendos and jokes in mixed company are ever appropriate in school and on your job, or whether you should be touching a woman in an obviously sexual way. Think twice before you act, and try to determine the motivation behind your behavior. Is it innocent? Are you trying to turn her or yourself on with a joke or a touch? Or are you trying to get attention, or show affection? Maybe you don't want to come off as a wimp, or be seen as a prude?

If you're a young woman, you will know when a sexual overture is welcome or not, and you may even know instinctively that the young man has gone too far, and that he is a letch. Yet you must also know what you have in mind when you dress a certain way or flirt. If a young man responds aggressively to something that you say or do, ask whether you were the one who went too far first. If your behavior wasn't exactly innocent, how far did you mean to go? Were you trying to strike up a romantic relationship, or were you just teasing?

While women often do have some control over the responses of men and bear responsibility for some instances of sexual harassment, the stereotypes about women that men grow up with are far more responsible for the abuse directed against women. And one that has to be dispelled is that women are entitled to less respect than men, that there's nothing wrong with their being subjected to sexual commentary from a male who needs to use them as playthings.

THE DOUBLE STANDARD

Rape and battery are the severest forms of sexism against women. For their sheer violence and the lasting effects they have on a woman, nothing else that men do to women can compare. Sexual harassment can fill a woman with great fear, especially in cases when she knows that if she does not endure it she could be fired. Each of these forms of abuse has its roots in prejudice toward women.

There is, however, yet another kind of prejudicial behavior directed against women, one that causes deep resentment, emotional anguish, and often economic hardship. It is the kind of bias that grows out of the double standard, that unwritten rule that says that what's okay for a man isn't okay for a woman.

We say *unwritten* because such a view isn't generally stated in our laws — at least not anymore. But it used to be. For instance, more than a century ago, the U.S. Supreme Court turned down a woman's claim that a state could not bar women from practicing law. Judge Joseph Bradley wrote:

> Man is, or should be, woman's protector and defender. The natural and proper timidity and delicacy which belongs to the female sex evidently unfits it for many of

> the occupations of civil life. The constitution of the family organization, which is founded in the divine ordinance, as well as in the nature of things, indicates the domestic sphere as that which properly belongs to the domain and functions of womanhood. The harmony, not to say identity, of interests and views which belong or should belong to the family institution is repugnant to the idea of a woman adopting a distinct and independent career from that of her husband. . . . The paramount destiny and mission of woman are to fulfill the noble and benign offices of wife and mother. This is the law of the creator.[9]

"Boo, hiss," you might well say. But the judge's words reflect the attitudes of his time. Most men living then agreed with those sentiments — and, unfortunately, so, too, would some of today's men. For years women were either not allowed to work at all or exploited in firetrap, sweatshop garment factories and paid appallingly low wages for working up to seventy-five hours a week.

Once, women were not allowed to vote anywhere, including in the United States, a carryover from the days when soldiers, kings, and emperors alone governed and not the people. Later, voting by ballot came along, but its use was restricted to men who owned property, to the clergy, and to noblemen. In Colonial New England, where children, property, and money belonged only to the husband, statutes barred women from voting. Besides owning property, men eligible to vote had to belong to the established Protestant church, or they had to be taxpayers or be educated. Barred on any account, along with women, were Indians, blacks, criminals, transients, and "lunatics and idiots." Eventually, property and religious requirements were dropped, but suffrage, or the right to vote, was still a male privilege and for many years only for white males. It took seventy years of agitation, marches, and other demonstrations for women to finally win the right to vote in several countries. The United States was among the last countries to confer the right to women, with the adoption of the Nineteenth Amendment to the Constitution in 1920.

Among the leaders in the women's suffrage movement was Susan B. Anthony, a Quaker schoolteacher who was active in the anti-slavery movement and strongly believed in coeducation. What she had to endure from men underlines the lowly status of women in the early days of our country. In 1852, she was prevented from speaking at a women's rally against drinking because of her sex. And in 1872, before city officials could stop her, she voted illegally in the presidential election in Rochester, New York. Anthony was arrested, put on trial, and found guilty by an unfriendly judge who did not even bother to consult the jury. Fined one hundred dollars, she refused to pay, declaring, "Resistance to tyranny is obedience to God." It wasn't until fourteen years after her death that the Nineteenth Amendment was passed, the realization of her years of exhausting speechmaking throughout the country for women's voting rights. There is a sad, perhaps expected, sidelight to her story. In 1972, the U.S. Government minted a dollar coin with Anthony's profile engraved on it. Unfortunately the coin is almost the same size as a quarter — and it is hardly ever seen in circulation because people are afraid they might inadvertently use it in place of the twenty-five-cent piece. It is almost as though Susan B. Anthony is still kept out of sight.

Women vote throughout the world today, and no one would dare to write such a stern and biased legal decision as Judge Bradley's these days. But sex discrimination persists nonetheless. It persists quite noticeably in the workplace, where just about everywhere on earth women tend to hold less important jobs than men and are paid less. In South Korea and Cyprus, and in Japan, the economic giant of Asia and a formidable global power, women's wages are among the lowest in the world — half that of men.[10] In many parts of the world, women are also denied equal educational opportunities and health care. According to recent reports on the status of women by the United Nations, the World Health Organization, and the Older Women's League:

- Women work at least thirteen hours more than men every week in Asia and Africa.
- They hold only 10 to 20 percent of all manager's positions throughout the world.
- Women do not always have equal access to education, and there are almost 600 million illiterate women in the

world, compared with around 350 million illiterate men.

- Older women face even more bias in the workplace. The median annual earnings of American women forty-five to fifty-four years old have been around $20,000, or nearly 60 percent of the earnings of men the same age; women fifty-five to sixty-four earned $18,000, 57 percent of the earnings of men. Moreover, mocking, stereotypic images of older women contribute to their plight. One full-page advertisement for a major store chain depicts a young woman sitting at a computer. The caption reads, "The difference between me and my mother? She still thinks software is a nightgown."[11]
- Women in many parts of the world do not get the same health care as men, and as a result they are more prone to disease. AIDS, for one, has become the leading cause of death for women age twenty to forty in major cities in the Americas and sub-Saharan Africa. Women in those countries are not given enough health information and have little or no voice in sexual matters. "Even though AIDS prevention strategies have included a wide range of components such as education, counseling, surveillance, testing, and research," the World Health Organization says, "they have yet to address the underlying problem of women's subordination as a factor in the epidemic. The subordinate position of women in the family and in society differs in detail and in degree from country to country, but its impact is similar everywhere, resulting in a social vulnerability to infection."[12]

Whether they are qualified or not, women are also barred outright from certain occupations, are not encouraged to pursue others, or make up only a small percentage of jobs not considered female occupations. Women cannot fight with infantry units in a war. They do not play on professional baseball, football, hockey, or basketball teams, nor do they referee or umpire. They make up a relatively small percentage of engineers, scientists, and airline pilots. They rarely become auto mechanics, welders, electricians, bricklayers, cabdrivers, or plumbers. The way we refer to some occupations also shows their traditional dominance by males: fisherman, lobsterman, telephone lineman, helmsman, doorman, handyman, plowman, fireman, repairman, sideman, brakeman. The fact that many women have held men's jobs during wartime should dispel any notion that women are not physically equipped to handle "men's work."

To our list we might add that women are barred from joining certain golf and social clubs, and when they are allowed in as visitors, they must follow discriminatory rules. I recall attending a meeting at an exclusive Boston club recently and being told that my wife had to enter through a separate door and that once inside, she could not even enter, let alone sit, in certain "male-only" rooms. One woman lawyer wrote recently of a country club on Long Island that allows women to eat in the main dining room, but not to sit in chairs with arms — these are reserved for men![13]

Such restrictions once a woman "gets inside" seem too ridiculous to be taken seriously in the twentieth century, yet they continue to exist nonetheless. Even more offensive is the double standard that prevails once women are on the inside of some universities and corporations. The policy, sometimes, is "Let 'em in, but keep 'em down." Along with getting less money, women often are not promoted as readily as men. The U.S. Labor Department found recently that bias keeps women from advancing to higher positions beyond what is referred to nowadays as the "glass ceiling." A review of nine large companies revealed that each stopped women and minorities from getting past the "glass ceiling" by not providing training programs for these groups and by showing little concern for promoting them.

Women who hold faculty positions in universities also quite often find it difficult to become heads of sections or departments or to win promotions to the high rank of full professor. Indeed, women are often discouraged from entering the sciences because of biases (among both educators and parents of young girls) that the various fields are somehow unfeminine or because women supposedly lack mathematical skills. Girls, after all, get the dolls, while the boys get the chemistry sets. As a result, only around 15 percent of scientists and engineers are women, and few of those make it really big, and the percentage of women receiving Ph.D.'s in mathematics is around 20 percent.

Although more women are now admitted to medical schools in the United States — 50 percent of the entering classes in most schools — once they graduate, they find it difficult to crack the "old boy network" that leads to promotions, especially in surgery, and to avoid being the target of sexist remarks. One recent case that made headlines involved Dr. Frances Conley, a brain surgeon at Stanford Medical School who quit her professorship after twenty-five years at the school because, she charged, she was subjected to demeaning comments and sexist attitudes by male colleagues. Dr. Conley said she had to work in an environment in which faculty members used *Playboy* centerfolds to "spice up" lectures, where sexist comments were frequent, and where those who were offended were told to be less sensitive. "Those who administer my work environment at the present time," she wrote in an article that appeared in various newspapers, "have never been able to accept me as an equal person." Surgery, she said, is a male-dominated profession that reinforces the concept of male superiority to such a degree that, for some men, it stunts personal growth as well as their ability to adjust to society's changes. "The danger for the future of medicine, and I suspect business and law," Dr. Conley went on, "comes when one of these individuals, who may be gifted technically as a physician, lawyer or businessman, is assigned a position with authority over the professional lives of others."[14]

Responding to Dr. Conley's allegations, Dr. David Korn, the school's dean, said that the school "does not and will not tolerate inappropriate sexual behaviors or actions, for they degrade the learning and working environment of this institution," adding that he wanted the surgeon to stay on and that he did not think losing her would be good for the community. "We still have much work to do in changing attitudes, beliefs and behaviors within our profession, to eliminate bigotry and bias and to make the medical profession more hospitable and nurturing to its women and ethnic minority members," Dr. Korn said.[15]

Dr. Conley eventually withdrew her resignation after consulting with colleagues and being reassured that the school was taking steps to fight sexism. "I support these initiatives," Dr. Conley said, "because they get people to admit or realize that a problem exists. But I will be convinced of their value only when I see a more open atmosphere at the school, one in which people who speak up can do so freely without having their jobs or careers truncated."[16]

Dr. Conley's willingness to speak out publicly was an effective way to call attention to the double standard that is so often applied to women. Sometimes, though, a sledgehammer approach in the courts may be necessary, especially when the glass ceiling has to be shattered. A credit manager for Texaco, Janella Sue Martin, was one woman who crashed through the ceiling by instituting a sex-discrimination suit against her employer. A loyal employee for twenty-five years, she charged that she was passed over for promotion, which she had been promised, because of the company's favoritism toward men. In 1991, she sued, and she won: a Los Angeles jury ordered Texaco to pay her $20.3 million in lost pay and damages, and promote her to the management job she said she had been denied. "I've never heard of an award this big," said a spokeswoman for 9 to 5, an advocacy group for working women, "but I'm very encouraged by it. Unfortunately, it may be the only way to modify corporate behavior — that you'll pay through the nose if you don't treat people equally."[17]

Men may still feel they have "appropriated the work requiring skill and strength," as noted earlier, but cases like Martin's and that of every other achieving woman prove that men won't appropriate it for long. Women already do much of the heavy lifting and the outdoor labor in many countries. And the carts and plows they drag alongside oxen on farms in China and Russia, the rice they plant and harvest, the corn they grind, and the animals they slaughter are proof — despite the fact that sometimes such work can be viewed as lowly, traditional occupations for women — that they can handle the rough stuff as well as men.

In fact, women have been making important contributions throughout history, but their achievements do not always draw the same attention as those of men. For example, even though some women astronaut-candidates performed better in endurance tests than male colleagues, they were not allowed in the space program until recently. In 1972, as reported by writer Gloria Steinem in the *New York Times*, a space agency official's view of a woman's function in space was "sexual diversion" on long-duration flights, such as to Mars.

Many achieving women are known only to women's groups, or they do their work quietly, with none of the publicity that men often draw. How many of us ever heard of Henrietta Hall Shuck of Virginia, the first American woman missionary to China in the early 1800s? Or Ella Flagg Young of Illinois, who in 1920 was the first woman elected president of the powerful National Education Association?

Other women have been more highly visible. There was Amelia Earhart, known as "The First Lady of the Air" and "Lady Lindy" (after the famed aviator Charles Lindbergh, first to fly solo across the Atlantic). Earhart was a famous aviator, the first woman to fly alone across the Atlantic (in 1932) and the first person to solo from Honolulu to the U.S. mainland. (Earhart and her copilot were lost somewhere in the South Pacific in 1937 while trying to fly around the world.) There was Dorothea Dix, who crusaded to change the appalling conditions in which mentally ill patients lived; Eleanor Roosevelt, wife of President Franklin D. Roosevelt, who became a national heroine and the "First Lady of the World" for her untiring efforts on behalf of the poor, women's rights, and better working conditions; and Marie Curie, the Polish-born French physicist who, with her husband, Pierre, investigated radioactivity, discovered radium, and shared a Nobel Prize in 1903.

Today women pilot jetliners, orbit the earth in shuttles, and serve as presidents and prime ministers of several countries. They function admirably, though fewer in number than men, as physicists and mathematicians and astronomers, soldiers and surgeons and police officers, TV anchors and TV technicians. There is really very little that men do that women cannot do, no matter what the guys down on the corner or the farm tell you.

Women represent more than 10 percent of the people in the army, navy, air force, and marines — a sizable number. During the Gulf War, some 35,000 women served in the armed forces in the battle zone. They tended the sick and wounded as nurses, flew cargo planes and troop-carrying helicopters, drove trucks, and operated computers that fired missiles and tracked enemy troop movements and missiles. Women were killed in the war, and they were captured by the enemy.

But women are not allowed to fight with ground forces or serve aboard fighting ships and submarines. This is a thorny issue and has been fiercely debated in Congress. The House of Representatives and the Senate have passed bills that would permit, but not force, women to fly warplanes in battle. And there have been suggestions that the law should be expanded to allow women to fight on the ground with infantry soldiers. Whether this will ever come about is uncertain.

The arguments, as expected, revolve around one's ideas about women's roles. General Robert H. Barrow, retired commandant of the Marine Corps, has offered what might be considered the majority view in the debate.

> Combat is finding, closing with, and killing or capturing the enemy. It's killing. And it's done in an environment that is often as difficult as you can possibly imagine. Extremes of climate. Brutality. Death. Dying. It's uncivilized! And women can't do it. Nor should they even be thought of as doing it. The requirements for strength and endurance render them unable to do it. And I may be old-fashioned, but I think the very nature of women disqualifies them from doing it. Women give life, sustain life, nurture life. They don't take it.[18]

That's one side of the argument. Advocates for women in combat can point to many examples of women who have fought against an enemy: women who defended themselves and their children against Indians on the American frontier, those who took up arms in the American Revolution, guerrilla fighters from many countries who participated in battles against government troops.

Understandably, those who are in favor of allowing women combat roles raise a number of questions. Why shouldn't women be allowed to fight if they are willing and able to? Isn't it a clear case of discrimination if they are forbidden to do so? Does the military have the right to act as a parent? Do the physical differences between men and women justify keeping women out of battle? If women can join the police force and carry guns, and sometimes engage in shootouts with criminals, why can't they serve in wartime combat? And last, should a woman in the service have any choice at all about whether she sees combat? Men don't.

Difficult questions to answer. But even if there is no easy answer about a woman's role in the military, it is clear that women, like men, make excellent workers, leaders, scientists, athletes, scholars. Their style might be different — one study found that women leaders tend to be more apt to collaborate and share in decision making than men, who tend to be more autocratic — but they get the job done. "People tend to be skeptical that women can do the job of leadership and particularly are distrustful of women who have masculine leadership styles or who occupy highly male-dominated roles," said psychologist Alice H. Eagly of Purdue University, who conducted the study. "Yet, women do quite well in leadership roles and are at least as effective as their male counterparts. In fact, subordinates are somewhat more satisfied with female than male leaders, suggesting that people often find that women are nice people to work for."[19]

In fairness, we should point out that sometimes women criticize men unfairly, even stereotype them. Men have been portrayed in television commercials and movies as stupid or insensitive, and some men are speaking out against such characterizations. But even though male-bashing exists, it is nowhere near as widespread as woman-bashing is.

We can end with a comment by Susan B. Anthony. It provides much food for thought the next time one is tempted to discriminate against a woman:

> Are women persons? I hardly believe any of our opponents will have the hardihood to say that they are not. Being persons, then, women are citizens; and no state has a right to make any law, or enforce any old law, that shall abridge their privileges or immunities.[20]

8 • HOMOPHOBIA
A Deadly Social Disease

If a man lies with a male as with a woman, both of them have committed an abomination; they shall be put to death; their blood is upon them.
— Leviticus 20:13

If a gay can win, it means there is hope that the system can work for all minorities if they fight.
— Harvey Milk, the first avowed homosexual to be elected to San Francisco's Board of Supervisors, who was murdered in City Hall in 1978

The Bible and Harvey Milk. The first takes the traditional view that only in marital relationships between men and women can sexual activity be considered moral. Milk disagreed that homosexuality was immoral and believed that being gay would not be held against him. "If I do a good job," he said not long before he was killed by a man who hated gays, "people won't care if I'm green or if I have three heads."

Milk was wrong. Some people do care if people are different, no matter how good they are at what they do. As we have seen, virtually every ethnic group in America has experienced prejudice firsthand, for the mere reason that they were unlike the majority.

This chapter does not deal with the reasons some people are homosexual, that is, why some men are sexually attracted to men and some women to women. Nor with whether homosexuality is a condition that can and should be cured. We covered those aspects of homosexuality in an earlier book, *Like, Love, Lust.* Suffice it to say here that homosexuality has been called everything from learned behavior to a hormone deficiency to a mental or moral weakness. What we are concerned with here is the prejudice against gays, with why some straight people hate or fear them so much. We hope to make it clear that this kind of prejudice is as unjustified and as serious as discrimination against any ethnic or racial group.

Some 25 million Americans are believed to be gay. They represent every ethnic and racial group, every religion. There are gay doctors and gay cops, gay Congressmen and gay professional football players, and gay brokers, bankers, and chairmen of company boards. Gays are also roofers and plumbers, carpenters and members of the clergy, and some are married. Some gay men are effeminate, others macho. Some gay women are quite feminine, others not so. Some gays are sexually promiscuous; others stay with a single partner all their lives. Some are guilty and depressed about their life-style and want to stop being gay, but most are happy with their sexual orientation and are no more psychologically unbalanced than non-gays. Some are more visible as they lobby for gay rights, marching in gay parades, protesting in churches and at city halls. Others do not participate in the marches, preferring to do their jobs quietly, stay at home with friends or family, and never admit they are gay, mostly because homosexuals are still not totally accepted by mainstream society.

If there is any correct way to describe a city's gay community the word is diverse. As one gay male told me, "It's not possible to stereotype a gay, except for the sexual preference. It's important to remember that the gay community is as diverse as the straight community in both sexual matters and in appearance. We see some pretty strange-looking straight people walking around these days, too."[1]

Because most gays don't have spouses or children, they have more leisure money, which has earned them a reputation as America's most affluent minority. Their often comfortable lifestyles, their enormous influence on the arts in America, and their generally quiet behavior allow them to participate more fully in society than, say, blacks who have been far more militant. Many people are not biased against gays, have normal relationships with them, and support their civil rights.

There are those, however, who are homophobic, that is, they are fearful of gays, a fear that translates into hatred. Some homophobics believe that gays are destroying the nation's morals; others are hostile toward gays because that is how they reassure themselves about their own heterosexuality.

Unfortunately, while there is widespread acceptance of gays — or at least disinterest — hostility toward them is increasing throughout the country. In fact, some gays feel that the black civil rights movement, with all of its ups and downs, has fared far better than the drive for gay rights. Incidents of violence against gays — ranging from physical assault to bomb threats to outright murder — have mounted over the past few years. When gays aren't being actually beaten up, they are harassed and ridiculed on the streets or sometimes treated badly by police.

The AIDS epidemic has worsened anti-gay feelings. Many people still believe that homosexuality causes the disease, that gays are to be avoided because they can infect non-gays, and that if it were not for gays, the world would not be dealing with this plague. All of these charges are wholly untrue, but they have fueled the already high level of gay bashing. It is true that when AIDS, the blood-borne disease that has killed many thousands of people here and abroad, first erupted more than ten years ago, its prime victims in the U.S. were gay men. This was because a sexual practice common among some gay men, anal sex, created breaks in the delicate membrane lining the rectum; the AIDS virus, which travels very fast when it gets into blood, was thus able to infect the gay men easily when it got into the injured rectum in sperm. The virus did not begin in homosexuals, but in an African monkey, and it somehow changed enough, as do many animal viruses, to be able to infect humans. Because some members of the gay community were promiscuous, that is, they had many partners, they infected many other gays, who infected others. But an infection with AIDS comes about through the exchange of various bodily fluids, usually blood. That is why drug abusers who shoot dope with shared needles are the second largest group of AIDS-infected people in the United States. Cases among gays have dropped dramatically over the last few years as more gays practice safe sex.

AIDS does not automatically go with sexual preference. To

have AIDS, a gay person must have done something that infected him or her, and that something is either anal sex, in the case of men, or using an AIDS-contaminated needle, or, as has happened to many straight people, after receiving tainted blood in a transfusion. And nonsexual contact with a gay person who is infected with AIDS does not lead to certain infection. There is no way a person can get AIDS from shaking hands with a gay person, whether the gay person is infected or not. We cannot get AIDS from plates served us by gay waiters, nor from toilet seats, doorknobs, swimming pools, sneezes, or letters. And yet some people still refuse to go near gay people because they fear they'll get AIDS. In New York City, some people refused to touch the campaign literature of a gay man running for City Council. In San Francisco, someone carried the phobia to a most disturbing extreme. He or she spray-painted the words "Prevent AIDS: kill a faggot" on the sidewalk outside a theater where a gay film was playing.

Prejudice against gays can be found in organizations as well as in individual members of society. One glaring example is found in the military. The U.S. Department of Defense bars gay men and lesbians from serving in the armed forces, and the only way they can remain in the service is to keep silent about their sexual preference. When gays are discovered in the military, they are discharged. And there quite a few of them: between 1950 and 1970, up to 50,000 people were discharged for homosexuality; 20,000 were released between 1974 and 1985; and since the beginning of 1990, at least 360 were discharged. If the government were able to enforce the rule fully, about 60,000 to 200,000 people now serving would be released.[2]

The military's justifications for trying to keep gays out of the service are quite discriminatory. Some arguments are that homosexuals may be poor security risks, more apt to be blackmailed, and unwilling to obey rules and regulations. Another is that gays may be emotionally unstable. Still another is that their presence in the military, particularly of gay men, is bad for the services' image, that is, because some gay men supposedly don't look truly manly, the macho image of the military would be watered down.

Every one of the above reasons has been challenged by social scientists who found that the Defense Department's policy on homosexuality is not based on any scientific data whatsoever but only on prejudice. Homosexuality is not a psychiatric disorder, gays are no more apt to be unpatriotic and security risks than any other people, and they are as dedicated to their work as anyone else. "Gay people have been in the armed forces for a long time," psychologist Michael Kauth of the University of Mississippi told a 1991 meeting of the American Psychological Association. "It is time to recognize their contribution, accept their presence and utilize them as valid resources, especially in today's shrinking labor pool. It does not make sense to exclude and separate persons based on a factor unrelated to job performance."[3]

The military is not, of course, the only group that tries to exclude homosexuals. Many parents and school committees are not happy about homosexuals teaching children — gays are either child molesters or corrupters of kids' morals, according to the rhetoric one hears in some communities — and some communities have succeeded in having gay teachers dismissed. Some companies once publicly refused to hire gays, and the Federal Civil Service Commission once ruled that gays were unfit for public service. The Boy Scouts of America barred homosexuals from joining until 1991, when they bowed to pressure from gay rights groups and the United Way in San Francisco and compromised by establishing a separate youth program for gays, atheists, and girls. (The irony about the Boy Scouts case is that the organization was founded in 1907 by Lord Robert S. S. Baden-Powell, a British Army officer who was reportedly a repressed homosexual.)

Not surprisingly, various churches have also taken anti-gay stances. Although individual priests and ministers within the churches are tolerant and make every effort to keep gays as members of the congregation, the leaders of some churches don't want gays as ministers and sometimes they don't even want them as parishioners unless they renounce their gay life-styles. The fact is, many members of the clergy and many parishioners are gay — one estimate by gay groups is that up to 50 percent of Catholic clergymen are — and, as in the military, little can actually be done about it unless the person goes public. When there is an admission, however, the churches invoke traditional policies that ban homosexuals from ordination, and they often shun openly gay parishioners.

The Vatican has long condemned homosexual activity as a sin and characterized even a tendency toward homosexuality as an "objective disorder." Priests have been disciplined by the Catholic church for permitting homosexual groups to hold special masses or for tolerating and accepting them in other ways. The gay groups themselves have been barred from using church schools or church halls for religious services or meetings. The late Humberto Cardinal Medeiros, the archbishop of Boston, once summed up his Church's views on homosexuality this way:

> According to the objective moral order, homosexual relations are acts which lack an essential and indispensable finality. In Sacred Scripture they are condemned as a serious depravity and even presented as the sad consequence of rejecting God. This judgment of Scripture does not, of course, permit us to conclude that all those who suffer from this anomaly are personally responsible for it, but it does attest to the fact that homosexual acts are intrinsically disordered and can in no case be approved.[4]

The Episcopal church, too, has had to address the gay issue, along with the various branches of the Jewish faith. Both religious groups also have leaders and members who condemn homosexuality, and they both have people who feel homosexuals have a place in the congregation. In 1991, the Episcopal Bishop of Washington, D.C., ordained a lesbian to the priesthood. Although she was not the first homosexual to be ordained by the Episcopal church (a gay male was ordained in Newark, New Jersey, in 1989, and another lesbian ordained in New York in 1977), the action created heated debate. Shortly afterward, the church's hierarchy approved a compromise resolution which, although it still technically banned the ordination of sexually active homosexuals (the church will ordain gays who have not made a public admission), it implied that such ordinations could be expected to continue and will probably increase. Many church leaders felt the compromise meant bishops could follow their own conscience in the matter, as the bishops who had ordained gays had done.

Generally, people who are prejudiced do not look upon the people they hate as individuals. They dislike every one of them, period. They tar them all with the same brush. All blacks are lazy, all Jews are greedy, all Italians are members of the Mafia, all Swedes and Poles are stupid. Most people who dislike homosexuals do not make any distinction between them as persons either. They hate all gays because, the reasoning goes, they are all sinners.

Interestingly, however, the bias against homosexuals is often selective. That is, sometimes one person or another will accept homosexuality, or ignore it, so long as the homosexual is celibate or has but a single lover or is a bisexual, that is, has an interest in both sexes. Other people like some homosexuals because they don't wear their sexual preference on their sleeves. Still others like some gays because they have gotten to know them, and they do not let their new friends' private sexual behavior interfere with that friendship.

If you are heterosexual and you make an effort to look at the whole person — and that can be a person whose color or ethnic background as well as sexual preference is disturbing to you — you have taken a giant step toward eliminating prejudice. In the case of homosexuality, you may still regard homosexual behavior as a sin, as is your right, but you can separate the "sin" from the "sinner." It takes courage and understanding to take such a stance and a willingness to weigh a person's good qualities and behavior against what you consider his or her negative ones. You'll also have to look inside yourself and ask yourself how you'd feel if the world were gay and you were a member of a heterosexual minority that was vilified, shunned, and sometimes even physically attacked.

Looking at the whole person requires, to say it once again, that you dismiss stereotypes. One study after another has demonstrated that all homosexuals cannot be lumped together, just as all heterosexuals are not the same. One important study, by scientists at the Institute for Sex Research, found that there are at least five types of homosexuality, each one with a different set of behavioral patterns. These patterns include "close couples," people who live like heterosexual married couples and are stable and contented; "open couples," who are less satisfied but looking for new partners; "functionals," or swinging singles who are sexually active, self-assured, and gregarious; "dysfunctionals," gays who are sexually active but less confident about their homosexuality; and "asexuals," gays who are not active sexually and regret their homosexuality. If you look carefully at those patterns, you'll see that some gays do fit the popular stereotype that gays are unhappy, unstable, and promiscuous — just as some heterosexuals are — but that others are like ordinary heterosexuals.[5]

Fortunately, many people, including legislators, understand this fact and also see that the injustice often directed against gays must be wiped out. Their arguments are persuasive. Gays have been denied health insurance, jobs, and promotions; they have been evicted from apartments because they are living with a lover; and they have been treated with extreme caution when they are hospitalized or have to see a doctor.

To correct some of the inequities, several states — Massachusetts, Connecticut, Hawaii, and Wisconsin among them — and many communities have passed gay rights legislation or give some legal protection to gays, who may be discriminated against in housing and state employment. In 1991, after an eighteen-year battle, Connecticut became the latest state to adopt a gay rights bill; it prohibits most landlords, banks, and employers from denying gays apartments, loans, and jobs. People who refuse to go along with the law can be penalized by a special commission on human rights. The courts, too, have addressed the gay rights issue. In 1969, the California Supreme Court ruled that homosexuality in itself was no reason to disqualify a teacher. Not long ago, the New York Supreme Court came up with a new legal definition of family that included homosexual couples; the court said that a gay couple who had lived together for ten years qualified as a family under the city's rent-control regulations.

The gay rights movement and the resulting legislation has, of course, raised some fears. Many people worry that too many changes will be made. For example, should gays be allowed to marry? Should a gay couple be allowed to adopt children? Should homosexual sexual behavior be included in sex education courses? Will gay rights laws and positive discussion about being gay spread homosexuality among young people? Beyond those questions is a much larger issue: would total acceptance, and encouragement, of homosexuality be destructive to the normal relationship between the sexes and, therefore, to the family as it is generally known throughout the world?

These are very difficult questions to answer, and they may not be answered to everyone's satisfaction for a long time. What we can say is that because homosexuality runs counter to a deep-rooted, indeed innate, instinct possessed by the vast majority of human beings — that is, the attraction between men and women — it is not possible that we will ever see the day when the world's population is transformed into a homosexual society. It may also be that society will never fully accept homosexuality, no matter how many laws are passed, no matter how much protest is raised by gay activists.

This does not mean that society has to stop caring about homosexuals. If you are not gay, it is important for you to see gays as human beings first. If you are uncomfortable with homosexuality, try to resist the impulse to lash out at gay people. Avoid what is known as an ad hominem attack: one that is based on your feelings or prejudices rather than on your intelligence. This is advice that can and should be applied to so many circumstances, from dealing with a person whose political or religious views are different from yours to dealing with minority groups.

If you cannot fully accept homosexuality, then try to apply some tolerance, the sort of tolerance that comes from making a real effort to understand, even sympathize with, another person's actions and beliefs. Too many people are fearful of tolerance because they think it implies that anything goes. It does not have to mean that. But you must make the choice about what to tolerate, and if you take the side of people who are not depriving you of your civil rights or injuring you in any way, and who are disliked only because they are different, then you are helping to put a stop to bigotry.

9 • OTHER "OUTSIDERS"
Imperfect in an Imperfect World

This is the law of the Yukon,
that only the Strong shall survive;
That surely the Weak shall perish,
and only the Fit survive.
— Robert William Service

It is hard to believe, but there is a form of prejudice that thrives on, and sometimes mocks, those who are physically, emotionally, or economically injured. These unfortunate people are often perceived as the damaged goods of our society, and as such they are often set apart or tossed out, just as broken or malfunctioning household appliances are.

Society's "outsiders" include the diseased and the mentally unbalanced, the physically disabled, the blind, the homeless, alcoholics and drug addicts, the aged, and the poor. They are people with AIDS and cancer, people in wheelchairs, productive grandfathers forced to retire before their time, mothers on welfare, bag ladies, men on the corner begging for your extra change, the armless, the legless, the mentally retarded neighbor, refugees fleeing a dictatorship. Even people who are fat or short are sometimes discriminated against when they look for jobs because a few employers reflect society's preoccupation with being thin or being tall and thus supposedly more "professional." It has also been suggested that short people are sometimes paid less than their taller co-workers, a practice which, if true, is not only grossly unfair but also ignorant and illegal.

There are other "imperfect" people in our midst, too, the ones who are made to feel flawed by the blessed and self-blessed: the "plain" woman who does not look like the *Playboy* centerfold, the person with a double chin or a large nose, the person who is forgetful, the C-student, the poor dancer, people "you can dress up but can't take anywhere."

The word *outsider* thus covers a broad range of people. But whether one is actually disabled or made to feel so, each must suffer at the hands of callous, arrogant, stupid people. These hapless men and women who are so "different" are routinely discriminated against, made to feel unwanted, even ridiculed — all because they are imperfect in an imperfect world.

Most of us have been guilty of such discrimination at one time or another, and with varying degrees of intensity. How many Helen Keller jokes have you chuckled over or told? How many times have you complained because the only open parking spaces in the supermarket lot were marked for the handicapped? Have you ever called a young woman a dog or a young man a wimp? Are you impatient with old folks? Do you try to communicate with your mentally retarded neighbor, or do you imitate him or her and wait for the laughs? Do you speak sharply to the guy looking for a handout? Do you believe that people with AIDS deserve what they got because many of them are drug abusers or homosexuals? Do you make fun of drunks? Have you stopped talking to the man next door since he lost his job and now shops with food stamps? Do you ask blind people if they'd like help crossing the street, or do you just walk around them and let them fend for themselves? Do you avoid people who are seeing a psychologist or psychiatrist? Or, worse, tell everyone that they're "nuts"?

Like all discrimination, discrimination against the disabled is not a new phenomenon. It has occurred for centuries, and in every culture. Sometimes it was accompanied by drastic acts. In ancient Greece, deformed children were hurled to their deaths from mountaintops; some African tribes buried the deaf and mute alive because they were supposedly possessed by evil spirits; the Nazis under Adolf Hitler not only massacred Jews but executed the mentally ill and those suffering from incurable diseases as well. In China today, mentally retarded people are prevented from marrying unless they are sterilized so they cannot bear children; if they become pregnant, they are forced to submit to abortions.

Few cultures go as far today to get rid of the disabled, preferring to practice the kind of good-riddance that relies on avoidance. "Out of sight, out of mind" is the expression. And so the disabled are often kept out of the workplace, shunned, or grudgingly thrown a favor every so often.

While out of sight may mean out of mind, the disabled people who are ignored remain with us, lonely and sometimes depressed, forced to go it as best they can with what strength they have. And that should not be.

One glaring example of how the disabled, and even their offspring, are discriminated against comes from Japan. It is a story that not too many Americans are aware of, and it has to do with the survivors of the atomic bombs that the United States dropped on Hiroshima and Nagasaki at the end of World War II. There are some 370,000 survivors, known in Japanese as *hibakusha.* They are physically, emotionally, and socially scarred, unable to obtain work and proper health care. They are damaged goods, members of a society that reveres perfection. Even the survivors' children have a hard time. Many cannot find good jobs or even marriage partners because many Japanese believe they will taint their children with the radiation damage suffered in the bomb blasts. Like rape and sexual harassment victims, many *hibakusha* do not admit to their plight and suffer silently because of the discrimination.

America does not have atomic bomb survivors, but we do have many people who have been injured in accidents or disfigured and crippled by disease. These people find it very difficult to get the right work, even though their minds may be first-rate. Sometimes, just having a disease such as cancer, ulcers, or diabetes can make an employer or health insurer wary of a job applicant, even though that person may not show any outward signs of the illness.

Sometimes the arguments given by those who discriminate against sick and disabled individuals seem to make sense. Employers worry that some illnesses might force the employee to take too many sick days off or that the employee won't be able to handle the pressure of a given job. Employers are also reluctant to pay for costly health insurance for people with serious illnesses. There are also explanations of why many restaurants, theaters, and stadiums do not provide accessible entry and seating for the disabled: wheelchairs, for example, could block doorways and prevent escape in the event of a fire; a person on crutches would not be able to move as fast in an emergency and would hinder others. Small commuter airlines would rather not accept people in wheelchairs for similar reasons.

But while each of these arguments must be considered, employers and the operators of various facilities can make changes if they really want to. Employers can evaluate a worker's ability and productivity instead of jumping to stereotypic conclusions about what having a certain disease means. Many of the diseases that frighten off employers can be controlled with medications that enable the patient to work normally, even for many years. Just having one should never be a reason to reject an employee. It is the same with the elderly or people who have had emotional difficulties. The elderly, as we pointed out in a previous book for young adults, *Growing Older,* are among the most discriminated-against people in America. The fact that many of them are productive well into their later years and therefore are a good investment for employers makes no difference to some employers. Employers routinely rid themselves of older employees or refuse to hire them when they have passed a certain age, sometimes as early as fifty. Of course, there are laws against such practices, but there are also ways around the laws: an employer might argue that a person is "overqualified" for a position, or that the employee makes "too much money" for the company to afford, or that the job "had to be abolished." All of these arguments are thin pretexts to cover up age discrimination.

Mental retardation — what generations of people used to call feeblemindedness — is another "illness" that turns off employers as well as the people next door. Retardation is not a mental illness. People afflicted with it merely learn slower than other people, and they do not absorb the same amount of knowledge. But the myth is that the retarded cannot learn. The retarded can learn, and they can work. How much they do of either depends solely on how much and what kind of effort is made by those who care enough for them.

Outside the workplace, there is room for much more to be done for the disabled. Fire laws make good sense and must be obeyed, but clubs and restaurants could stop jamming so many chairs and tables together; theaters could widen aisles and install ramps. Small airlines can use special hydraulic lifts, something like the ones larger commercial planes use, to board disabled passengers; they can install fewer seats in the planes or provide an area that can be broken down to accommodate a chair-bound passenger. These things are generally not done because they either are too costly or mar the appearance of a building's interior.

We should remember that each one of us has some handicap or other, a real one or one that someone has attached to us. This will make it easier to accept, and maybe even ignore, another person's disability. We can also be certain that just about every handicap can be compensated for, even if it can't be eliminated. People with disabilities of all kinds survive, and many of them function nearly as well as those more fortunate. President Franklin D. Roosevelt was crippled by polio and confined to a wheelchair; musicians Stevie Wonder, George Shearing, and Ray Charles are blind; movie and television actress Marlee Matlin is deaf; the late New York governor Nelson Rockefeller suffered from dyslexia, a reading disorder.

Many years ago, mystery writer Ernest Bramah created a blind detective named Max Carrados. Carrados was an ingenious creation, a man whose blindness is not a handicap but an advantage because it helps him sharpen his other senses to such an extent that he can even identify people before they speak, smell their clothes and tell what they are wearing from a distance, and hear things that other people cannot — something like what the English author John Lubbock meant when he said, "Milton in his blindness saw more beautiful visions, and Beethoven in his deafness heard more heavenly music, than most of us can ever hope to enjoy."

John Milton and Beethoven each had disabilities. Had they given up because of them, or been prevented from doing their work because of discrimination, they would not have given us, and themselves, so much pleasure.

10 • CONCLUSION
America's Ever-Changing Mosaic

Can we all get along?
— Rodney King

As we conclude our discussion of prejudice and discrimination, let's consider one last maligned group, the Wisians. Have you heard of these people? What do you think of them? If you were asked to rate their social standing in the U.S. — rank them, say, against Irish, Italians, Asians, Jews, African-Americans, and Hispanics — where would you put them? High on the list, or way down low?

Judging from the results of a recent nationwide poll that asked people to rank the Wisians, a lot of Americans don't care much for them, and they wound up on the very bottom rungs of the social status ladder. Why? What have the Wisians done to be held in such low regard?

The fact is, the Wisians have never done anything to Americans or to anybody else in the world, and they have never been a threat to anyone. Wisians haven't been a bother for the simple reason that they don't exist.

The Wisians are a fictitious ethnic group. The name was added to the list of familiar racial and ethnic groups by the pollsters in order to determine whether the respondents were paying attention to the survey, how much they knew about ethnic groups, and what response a strange name would bring.

While more than 60 percent of the people who replied to the poll admitted they could not rank the social standing of Wisians, the rest did — and they placed the fake group thirty-fourth on a list of thirty-seven. (Grouped around the Wisians on the lowest end of the scale were American Indians and African Americans just above, and Mexicans, Puerto Ricans, and gypsies below.)

What is troubling about the place of the Wisians was the willingness of people to judge them without ever having heard of them. The name was enough to stereotype them. As the director of the survey, Tom W. Smith of the University of Chicago, explained it, "People probably thought that if (the Wisians) were foreign-sounding, and they never heard of them, they couldn't be doing too well."[1]

As we have seen throughout this book, prejudice and discrimination arise not only from a perceived threat from some group or other, or when the economy or the political structure falters and a scapegoat is needed, but from ignorance, from the fear of the unknown. That is why we have been saying that if prejudice is ever to be wiped out, all the myths and misconceptions, all the stereotypes about certain people, have to disappear first. And the only way we can rid ourselves of all those erroneous impressions is to learn more — and to really want to learn more — about the different ethnic, racial, and religious groups in our midst. If we take a genuine interest in others, in what they are and what they believe, and try not to judge them because they look, think, or act differently from us, then we can get along. We not only have to learn about cultural, ethnic, and religious differences, but we have to accept them and to praise them when praise is merited.

If we have a problem with that, we should dwell a bit on the adage about not doing to our neighbors what we would not want them to do to us. Each one of us, after all, has distinct racial, ethnic, and cultural roots, and we all want what is best about our respective cultures to be understood and credited. Some of us belong to cultures whose traditions are markedly different from the mainstream population, others share beliefs and practices similar to other groups, while still others seem to pay little attention to being anything but "American," whatever that is supposed to mean in a country like ours with such a wide variety of people living almost side by side.

We are, then, a mix, a combination that is often likened to a melting pot. But if the melting pot analogy were true, we probably wouldn't have as much prejudice and discrimination as we do now. The fact is, we really are more like a stew, or a mosaic, because the diversity does not really disappear as it would if everything were truly melted down and blended together. Each group's customs, language, and even foods, give it its special identity, and our immigrants and their descendants have preserved their cultures. American though many may be, they still stand out. It is this diversity that makes us — as the Latin inscription on our great seal, *E pluribus unum,* indicates — one people composed of many. America is strong because it can draw on the skills and ideas of so many different peoples working together under one flag. The immigrants and refugees who come here seeking freedom and a better way of life are essential parts of the whole, just as the different parts and materials of a machine make it run.

Total assimilation in a melting pot, whereby one sheds or forgets his or her ethnicity, is as unrealistic as it is undesirable. We cannot all be the same nor, I dare say, would we want to live in a country where that was the way it was. It might make for what the sociologists call social cohesion, but it would be a very boring way to live. And whether wiping out cultural heritages would mean a world totally free of prejudice is highly unlikely: even today, when there is so much hatred between groups, it is not uncommon for people of the same racial or ethnic group to be at odds with members of their own group for some reason or other.

But as desirable as our ethnic, racial, and religious mosaic is, it is obviously a factor behind the prejudice we have been reading about here. While maintaining one's ethnicity and racial ties can provide comfort, security, and friendship, it can also create difficulties. For too little assimilation — the process of being absorbed into a culture — stimulates racial and ethnic prejudice. Strongly ethnic groups stand out, and because they are so visible, they are discriminated against by those who do not belong to those groups. Moreover, when there is too much emphasis on racial and ethnic pride and on preserving every bit of one's heritage, the bonding that has made America what it is may be threatened. In a sense, there may be more emphasis on *pluribus* than on *unum,* more attention paid to our cultural diversity and not enough to what we share. Indeed, battles erupt regularly over whether to place foreign-language signs in public places and over whether English should be the only language taught in school. Some ethnic groups demand that examinations for public jobs, applications for everything from credit to telephone service, and tests for drivers' and professional licenses be offered bilingually; there have been efforts to change history textbooks and aptitude tests to include the experiences of nonwhites.

It is a dilemma that has no easy answer. On the one hand we are faced with the need for foreigners to integrate into American society, and on the other their need — and indeed, their duty — to exalt their own race and ethnicity. The only logical conclusion is that both points of view must be accepted. Not one but both.

The burden, then, is on each and every one of us. Not only immigrants but the sons and daughters, and the grandchildren, of immigrants. If you have just come to America, it is understandable that it will be difficult for you to place less emphasis on the ways of your own native country and pay more attention to America's. But while you must live and work and go to school here, you should not be expected to renounce your heritage. Even if you wanted to, you could not. It will be harder for you, as it has been for every immigrant, to live in two worlds, but you must try. If you are the offspring of immigrants, and born in the U.S.A., you should remember that your allegiance should be to your native country, but that does not mean you forget your roots and adopt purely "American" ways; be proud of who you are and where you came from, and don't ever apologize for it. We must learn to draw on the best of the different worlds that have shaped us, and we must understand that others are trying to do the same. In living with our ethnicity and our racial backgrounds, as in going through life in general, we should not try to live in the past, but we also should not lose sight of the past.

If we can appreciate that each one of us is a product of special cultures, if we can open our minds to the differences and still see that we are all, as they say, brothers and sisters under the skin, and if we renounce acts of racial and ethnic violence whenever they occur, then we will be able to live together. We have to do the right thing, not only because we may belong to the ethnic or racial majority living in a neighborhood that has a small minority of people unlike us, but because we may be a minority in some other neighborhood. We both have to learn to move over a little.

NOTES

1. RACE AND RACISM

1. Madison Grant, *The Passing of the Great Race* (New York: Charles Scribner's Sons, 1920) p. xi.
2. Ibid., p. 263.
3. Caroline Singer, "Race? What the Scientists Say," pamphlet. (Camden, N.J.: Haddon Craftsmen, 1939) p. 3.
4. "Is Vincent Sarich Part of a National Trend?" *Science* (January 25, 1991) p. 369.
5. H. E. Barnes and N. K. Teeters, *New Horizons in Criminology* (New York: Prentice Hall, 1943) p. 185.
6. Ibid.

2. AFRICAN-AMERICANS

1. Associated Press, "Survey Finds Whites Retain Stereotypes of Minority Groups," *New York Times* (January 1, 1991) p. B10.
2. Lewis Copeland, ed., *The World's Great Speeches* (New York: Garden City Publishing Company, 1942) p. 299.

3. *Universal History of the World,* Vol. 16, (New York: Golden Press, 1966) p. 1331.
4. Copeland, ed., *The World's Great Speeches,* p. 333.
5. Michael K. Frisby, "Gap Among Blacks Widening," *Boston Globe* (August 9, 1991) p. 1.
6. Randall Rothenberg, "Blacks Are Found to Be Still Scarce in Ads in Major Magazines," *New York Times* (July 23, 1991) p. A18.
7. Lena Williams, "When Blacks Shop, Bias Often Accompanies Sale," *New York Times* (April 30, 1991) p. 1.
8. Jerry Gray, "Panel Says Courts Are Infested with Racism," *New York Times* (June 5, 1991) p. B1.
9. David Margolick, "In Land of Death Penalty, Accusations of Racial Bias," *New York Times* (July 7, 1991) p. 1.
10. Harvey Araton, "Aaron Confers with Vincent on Remarks About Hiring," *New York Times* (May 12, 1991) p. B1.
11. Sue Armstrong, "Watching the Race Detectives," *New Scientist* (April 20, 1991) p. 61.
12. "Clarence Thomas, in His Own Words," *New York Times* (July 21, 1991) p. A14.
13. David Dinkins, "An Affirmation of Tolerance and Respect," address delivered in New York City, May 11, 1990.

3. RELIGIOUS PREJUDICE

1. Copeland, ed., *The World's Great Speeches,* p. 63.
2. Hendrick Van Loon, *The Story of Mankind* (Boni and Liveright, 1921) p. 173.
3. "Hostility Toward Arabs and Jews Is Found on the Rise," *New York Times* (February 7, 1991) p. A22.
4. Daniel J. Boorstin, *The Americans* (New York: Random House, 1958) p. 40.

4. JEWS

1. Martin Gilbert, *The Holocaust: A History of the Jews of Europe During the Second World War* (New York: Holt, Rinehart and Winston, 1985) p. 19.
2. Abram L. Sachar, *A History of the Jews* (New York: Alfred A. Knopf, 1964) p. 133.
3. Will Durant, *The Age of Faith* (New York: Simon and Schuster, 1950) p. 388.

4. Ibid., p. 388.
5. Sachar, *A History of the Jews,* p. 303.
6. Durant, *The Age of Faith,* p. 395.
7. Ibid., pp. 393–94.
8. Gilbert, *The Holocaust,* pp. 415–16.
9. B. M. Mooyaart, *Anne Frank: The Diary of a Young Girl* (New York: Random House, 1952) p. 65.
10. Henry Kamm, "Anti-Semitic Taunt at Wiesel Talk in Romania," *New York Times* (July 3, 1991) p. A8.
11. Associated Press, "Video Game Uncovered in Europe Uses Nazi Death Camps as Theme," *New York Times* (May 1, 1991) p. A10.
12. Robert Pear, "Thomas Expressed Admiration for Farrakhan," *New York Times* (July 13, 1991) p. 7.
13. Nat Hentoff, "God Must Have Loved Anti-Semites, He Made so Many of Them," *Village Voice* (May 7, 1991) p. 20.
14. Caroline Singer, "Race? What the Scientists Say," pamphlet. (Camden, N.J.: Haddon Craftsmen, 1939) p. 14.
15. Joel Brinkley, "Walesa, in Israel, Regrets Poland's Anti-Semitism," *New York Times* (May 21, 1991) p. A5.
16. A. James Rudin, "Chronic Ambivalence: Anti-Semitism in Europe," *Commonweal* (February 8, 1991) p. 86.

5. NATIVE AMERICANS

1. *Concise Dictionary of World History* (New York: Macmillan, 1983) p. 389.
2. John Bartlett, *Familiar Quotations,* 15th ed. (Boston: Little, Brown, 1980) p. 610.
3. Dee Brown, *Bury My Heart at Wounded Knee* (New York: Holt, Rinehart and Winston, 1970) p. 444.
4. Alan Thein Durning, "Native Americans Stand Their Ground," *Worldwatch* (November-December, 1991) pp. 11–12.
5. American Indian Relief Council flyer. (Rosebud Sioux Reservation, Little Soldier's Camp, South Dakota, 1991).
6. Copeland, ed., *The World's Great Speeches,* p. 267.
7. Ibid., p. 268.

6. IMMIGRANTS

1. "Ellis Island," U.S. Department of the Interior brochure (1990).
2. Kevin Sack, "Cuomo on Ethnic Types," *New York Times* (July 23, 1991) p. B4.

3. "The Ups and Downs of Making It in America," *Washington Post* (October 14, 1991) p. 20.
4. Nathan Glazer and Daniel Patrick Moynihan, *The Melting Pot* (Cambridge: MIT Press, 1970) p. 245.
5. Brett Howard, *Boston: A Social History* (New York: Hawthorn Books, 1976) p. 102.
6. "The Italian Contribution," *La Parola del Popolo: the USA Bicentennial* (1976) p. 125.
7. Ibid., p. 197.
8. Thomas Sowell, *Ethnic America* (New York: Basic Books, 1981) pp. 115–16.
9. Stephanie Bernardo, *The Ethnic Almanac* (New York: Doubleday, 1981) p. 346.
10. Wayne Moguin, ed., with Charles van Doren, *A Documentary History of the Italian-Americans* (Westport, Conn.: Praeger, 1975) p. 257.
11. Ray Bearse, ed., *Massachusetts: A Guide to the Pilgrim State* (Boston: Houghton Mifflin, 1971) p. 48.
12. H. E. Barnes and N. K. Teeters, *New Horizons in Criminology* (New York: Prentice Hall, 1950) p. 422.
13. "The Italian Contribution," p. 191.
14. Gwen Kinkead, "Chinatown," *The New Yorker* (June 10, 1991) p. 79.
15. Ibid.
16. Ibid.
17. Stephan Thernstrom, ed., *Harvard Encyclopedia of American Ethnic Groups* (Cambridge: Harvard University Press, 1980) p. 566.
18. "Blacks Attack Three Vietnamese," *New York Times* (May 14, 1990) p. 1.
19. Ibid.
20. Felicity Barringer, "Despite Some Hispanic Gains, Report Finds They Still Lag," *New York Times* (April 11, 1991) p. E10.
21. Christine Dugas, "Activists Accuse Banks of Race Bias in Lending," *New York Newsday* (October 5, 1991) p. 15.
22. Mary B. W. Tabor, "Judge Finds Bias Against Minority Inmates," *New York Times* (October 3, 1991) p. B1.
23. Georges Vernez and David Ronfeldt, "The Current Situation in Mexican Immigration," *Science* (March 8, 1991) p. 1189.
24. Ibid.
25. Ibid., p. 1192.
26. Thomas Wheeler, ed., *The Immigrant Experience* (New York: Viking, 1971) p. 94.
27. Ibid., p. 58.

7. Sexism

1. *New Standard Encyclopedia* Vol. 25. (New York: Funk and Wagnalls, 1934) p. 273.
2. Linda Tschirhart Sanford and Mary Ellen Donovan, *Women and Self-Esteem* (New York: Viking, 1984) p. 165; quoting Julia O'Faolain and Lauro Martines, *Not in God's Image* (New York: Harper and Row, 1973) p. 132.
3. Ibid.
4. Roger Burlingame, *The American Conscience* (New York: Alfred A. Knopf, 1957) p. 88.
5. Ray Bearse, ed., *Massachusetts: A Guide to the Pilgrim State* (Boston: Houghton Mifflin, 1971) p. 393.
6. Ibid.
7. E. R. Shipp, "Sex Assault Cases: St. John's Verdict Touches Off Debate," *New York Times* (July 25, 1991) p. B1.
8. Barbara Crossette, "Indian Women's Group Takes On Abuse Cases That Government Neglects," *New York Times* (May 3, 1991) p. A8.
9. Kenneth Karst, *Belonging to America* (New Haven: Yale University Press, 1989) p. 105.
10. Marvine Hone, "Sex Discrimination Persists, U.N. Says," *New York Times* (June 16, 1991) p. 7.
11. Tamar Lewin, "Older Women Face Bias in Workplace," *New York Times* (May 11, 1991) p. 8.
12. "AIDS and the Status of Women," World Health Organization news release (October 1990).
13. Norma Blumenfeld, "Now That Country Clubs Are Admitting Blacks . . . ," *New York Times* (August 29, 1990) p. A21.
14. "Stanford Neurosurgeon Withdraws Resignation," Stanford University Medical Center news release (September 4, 1991).
15. "Stanford's Medical Dean Discusses Resignation of Neurosurgeon Who Alleges Widespread Sexual Discrimination," Stanford University Medical Center news release (June 3, 1991).
16. "Stanford Neurosurgeon Withdraws Resignation."
17. Thomas J. Maier, "Jury Blasts Texaco," *New York Newsday* (October 5, 1991) p. 5.
18. Donald G. McNeil, Jr., "Should Women Be Sent into Combat?" *New York Times* (July 21, 1991) p. E3.
19. "Women Found to Be Effective Leaders Despite Different Leadership Styles," American Psychological Association news release (August 16, 1991).

20. Copeland, ed., *The World's Great Speeches,* p. 321.

8. HOMOPHOBIA

1. John Langone, "Just Plain Folks — And Gay," *Boston Herald American* (July 13, 1980) p. A9.
2. "Researchers Conclude That No Scientific Evidence Exists to Support DOD's Policy on Homosexuals," American Psychological Association news release (August 18, 1991).
3. Ibid.
4. Humberto Cardinal Medeiros, "Pastoral Letter," *Boston Herald American* (July 16, 1980) p. A9.
5. Patricia McCormack, UPI, "Study Finds Diversity, Stability in Gay Lifestyles," *Boston Herald American* (August 9, 1978) p. 12. Jane Brody, "Homosexual Study Claims Many Lead Stable Lives," *New York Times* (August 9, 1978) p. 11.

10. CONCLUSION

1. Tamar Lewin, "Study Points to Increase in Tolerance of Ethnicity, *New York Times* (January 8, 1982) p. A12.

INDEX